When it HURTS to Live

DEVOTIONS for Difficult Times

Kathleen Kern

F&L
FAITH & LIFE
PRESS

Newton, Kansas
Winnipeg, Manitoba

When It Hurts to Live: Devotions for Difficult Times

Published simultaneously in Canada by Faith & Life Press Canada, Winnipeg, Manitoba R3P 0M4.

Printed in the United States of America

97 96 95 94 4 3 2 1

Library of Congress Number 94-61647

International Standard Book Number 0-87303-233-0

Editorial direction for Faith & Life Press by Susan E. Janzen; copyediting by Mary L. Gaeddert; design by Paula Johnson; printing by Mennonite Press.

Contents

Acknowledgments

I wish first to acknowledge the Klassen family—Victor, Susan, Nathan, and Sylvia. There are no words strong enough in any language to express my gratitude for the family, home, and friendship they have shared with me during the development of this book. A simple thank-you is also in order for Victor and Sue's proofreading.

I wish to thank the Rochester Area Mennonite Fellowship for their support, especially Teresa, Darren, and Eileen for their input.

Thanks to Bob Lasher for acting as a sounding board and Susan Janzen who encouraged me to develop a glib idea into a book.

Finally, I wish to thank the Sisters of St. Joseph in Rochester, New York, who provided me with a retreat to pull this book together, and especially Sr. Anne Alderman, my spiritual director.

This book is dedicated to Anita Olson, Anne Alderman, and Marlene Dohr, who have walked with me parts of the way on my journey towards healing.

Introduction

The pastor of the church I attended as a child had a habit of running overtime while preaching. He typically made up the time by cutting short the hymn that followed the sermon.

One Sunday during Advent the final hymn was Henry Wadsworth Longfellow's "I Heard the Bells on Christmas Day." As was his custom, the pastor instructed the congregation to sing the first three verses only. Coming to the third verse, we sang:

> Then in despair I bowed my head
> There is no peace on earth, I said.
> For hate is strong and mocks the song
> Of peace on earth, good will to men.
> Amen.

This memory encapsulates the dilemma facing Christians who struggle with depression. The amen cuts in too soon, keeping us from the promise of resolution and hope for what seems like a long time.

We are faced with a continuing dreary reality, a persistent sadness, a dread of existence itself that even the grace of God cannot seem to penetrate.

Other Christians and our loved ones try to

help. They recommend Psalms that have helped them when they have felt a little blue. They remind us that we serve the risen Lord who told us not to be anxious. They tell us to praise God for our many blessings, for in doing so we will not focus so much on the negative aspects of our lives.

And we feel even worse. We do serve a risen Lord. We love God, who has showered us richly with blessings. We *have no right* to feel as despondent as we do. And yet we do feel sad, discouraged, and afraid. We berate ourselves for not having the faith that our lives will get better or that we will find meaning in them.

These devotions are for people who turn to the Bible when they need answers or guidance for the difficult periods in their lives. This book is intended for anyone who might find it helpful. However, I have written especially for those who suffer from prolonged depression. I have in mind those who have done all the right things to address their condition, who have sought counseling and spiritual guidance, who are tired of waiting for healing.

Depression is a medical condition caused by chemical imbalances in the brain that affect people's emotions, energy levels, sleep patterns, and ability to concentrate. These imbalances can result from one's genetic makeup and from physical and emotional trauma. Certain types of medication can correct these imbalances and enable people to resume their normal level of functioning.

Depression is also a psychological condition. Psychologists commonly refer to it as anger turned inward. Depression can result when people have not adequately dealt with issues from their past or have not successfully or honestly dealt with current stresses in their lives. Psychotherapy can help people analyze why they feel the way they do and offer guidance as people make the difficult decision to change.

Depression is also a spiritual condition. It is a feeling that God has deserted us, or that God for some reason chooses not to help us. It is a feeling of deep loneliness, a separation from the rest of humanity. It is a feeling of guilt that our faith is not strong enough to believe that we will be healed. It is guilt over our self-absorption, and guilt that our faith in Christ does not seem to be enough to make us happy. Pastoral counseling and the church community can offer support when people feel this way. Depressed members of the church can lean on the faith of others.

As more Christians enter the fields of psychiatry and psychotherapy, depression can be treated in a more wholistic manner than in the past. There are many Christian counselors and psychiatrists who address the medical, psychological, and spiritual aspects of the condition when people come to them for help.

However, a split still seems to exist between the secular world and the church community when discussing treatment of depression.

Secular counselors and psychiatrists, most of them loving and supportive people, cannot always address the spiritual aspect of depression. They can help Christians sort through issues and emotions that keep them from functioning as full human beings. But they may be unsure of how they can help someone struggling with feelings of desertion by God. In a worst-case scenario, they can dismiss someone's spirituality as part of his or her neurosis and lead him or her to an even more vast spiritual desert.

Pastors and other concerned Christians can sympathize with someone who experiences feelings of spiritual desolation. They can pray for healing and offer guidance from their experience and from their knowledge of Scripture. However, they can fail to acknowledge the medical and psychological aspects of depression. In a worst-case scenario, they can tell someone afflicted with depression that if they would just get right with God, they would not need antidepressant medication or psychotherapy. Thus, they place guilt as an additional burden on the already struggling believer.

Many Christian self-help books can evoke guilt as well. One well-known author says that continuing to give in to sorrow and tears not only disgraces oneself, one's friends, and one's loved ones, but that it also dishonors God. He goes on to write that God wants to be credited with giving us joy, not grief.

What does this teach Christians suffering from prolonged depression? First, it teaches them that if they would just decide not to be depressed anymore, their depression would end. If they continue to suffer depression after making the decision, they must not really want healing. Second, it teaches them that their depression makes other people miserable, especially the people who care most about them. If they can't just cheer up, they should stay away from other people until they do. Or, since their depression disgraces other people, and they can't seem to make it end, perhaps they should kill themselves. Third, it teaches them that God doesn't want to hear from depressed Christians until they shape up. They hurt God when they selfishly remain depressed. Again, depressed people might mistakenly conclude that they should stay away from other people until they can cheer up, or maybe they should kill themselves.

This author's books have helped millions of people at difficult times in their lives. However, cheery platitudes like "It takes guts to leave the ruts!" cannot always bring comfort to the Christian suffering from chronic depression. Such platitudes can make suffering seem trivial. Does the phrase "The cross is a minus turned into a plus" even begin to touch the terror and pain Christ felt during his crucifixion? Or for that matter, the profound miracle of his resurrection?

• • •

My own struggles with depression have taught me that it heals neither quickly nor easily and that the medical, psychological, and spiritual aspects of the disease all need treatment.

I have had three major episodes of depression. I sought and received help for the second and third episodes of depression. I did not call the first episode by that name until I had the advantage of hindsight. I was depressed from at least age twelve until I went off to college. I remember as a thirteen-year-old fervently praying to die. The request became a routine part of my prayers, along with requests to have no nightmares and to pass tests. When I went away to college, I experienced a great spiritual awakening. For the first time in my life I felt the presence of God as a living reality. For the first month or so of my freshman year, I felt so happy that I almost found it physically painful. Sometimes I thought my heart would explode with joy.

After I had calmed down somewhat, I realized that I was experiencing mere happiness of the sort most people experience. I had always assumed that most people wore their happiness as a front, as I had (when I had the strength to keep up a front). Now I knew the reality of happiness and realized how unhappy I had been. I learned that the depression I had felt for nearly half my life was not the real me. It was not what God wanted or expected of me.

My second bout with depression occurred as a result of a trauma in my life when I was twenty-five. As a result of this trauma, I ended up on a psychiatric ward for one week.

I hated every moment I was there. I didn't belong there, I told myself. I wasn't crazy. However, since the doctors would not let me go home, I made friends with two people on the ward, Scott and Avery (not their real names), who had also suffered traumas. Scott was a construction worker and ex-Marine whose wife had left, taking his kids with her. Avery was a convicted felon who hadn't been able to pull his life together after his family moved off one of the Native American reservations in upstate New York.

Avery had tried to commit suicide in prison three times. The authorities had stopped giving him silverware at meals, but he had discovered that he could unwind the metal tip of his shoelace and sharpen it on the concrete floor until it was sharp enough to slice through his wrist. Since Avery was still technically under custody during his weeks on the ward, a prison guard stayed with him at all times, silently following him from room to room.

Avery, Scott, and I talked for hours. We learned to ignore the guard. I would have felt nothing in common with them in the outside world. Yet we became a community on the ward, bound together by our common suffering. As the two of them chain-smoked, something I would not have ordinarily tolerated, we shared the hurts of our past and present more intimately than I have shared with most people in my church.

My time on the psych ward benefited me in several different ways. It taught me that I never wanted to go back there. It taught me to become less judgmental of people who were from different backgrounds. It taught me what it feels like to be treated like a child. (When I subsequently began to work with developmentally disabled adults, I remembered how humiliated I had felt by the way the orderlies had treated me. I conscientiously worked at not treating the people I worked with like children.) At the recommendation of one of the psychiatrists who had seen me there, I asked my doctor to prescribe antidepressants for me, which gave me the energy I needed to make it through each long and dreary day. Finally, the psych ward experience served as a springboard for long-term therapy with a sequence of Christian counselors.

Since that time I have done some counseling myself and realize now that I was the sort of client most therapists enjoy treating. I wanted to come to terms with the aspects of my past and present that fostered my depression, and I conscientiously followed my counselor's advice. Gradually, my appointments became fewer and farther between. Finally, I and the counselor I was seeing at the time agreed that I had successfully completed therapy.

My third experience with depression began a couple of years ago. I had become discouraged by political maneuverings at the agency where I worked. My dissatisfaction with work caused me to look to the future. I realized that I did not know what direction my life should take, and began to feel despair at the transience and lack of roots in my life. Since I had read all the right books and learned all the right ways to think, the most recent bout of depression came as an unpleasant shock. I had learned to count my blessings and put my suffering in perspective. I had learned how to build up my self-esteem. So, why, I wondered, was I feeling all the same stuff I felt before I had learned all the correct ways of thinking? How could self-loathing become so easily and deeply rerooted? What had caused the reincarnation of past traumas I thought I had dealt with completely in therapy?

I felt I had failed. Going on antidepressant medication again made me wonder if I had ever, in truth, really healed the first time. I wondered if the rest of my life would be characterized by periods of depression. Was I going to have to deal with the same old thing over and over again?

I probably will. And each time I do, I will be a little stronger and a little more able to bear it. Each time, I will bring to new episodes of depression the insights I gained during the last episode.

Each time, I will be better equipped to let God work through my depression and turn me into a better servant of God's kingdom.

• • •

I hope these devotions will address the reality of depression in the Christian life and will provide at least a small comfort to those afflicted by it.

I do not intend this book as a substitute for counseling or the support of a church community. I write from the perspective of a biblical scholar, not of a psychotherapist. My insights into depression come from personal experience. What caused your depression and what sort of help you need will differ from my experiences and treatments.

I would encourage any reader struggling with depression at this time to seek help from a pastor, counselor, or doctor. Don't hesitate to lean on the people who offer their help. You may have to go several routes before you find the person who can best help you manage your depression. Even if you feel overwhelmed by the small tasks of everyday living, try to summon up whatever initiative you have and get help. You owe it to yourself, to the people who care about you, and yes, to God, to move toward healing. Small steps towards getting help can mean a lot in the long run.

• • •

When I write Bible study curriculum for adults and young people, I ask myself certain questions so that I can better understand the Scripture texts. I look at the Greek or Hebrew text and see if any difficulties in translation exist. I examine the text's relationship to the rest of the biblical book in which it appears. I try to find out the historical situation in which the text was first written or in which it was collected in written form. I try to find out the audience for whom the text was originally intended.

Only when I have explored the situation the Scripture text spoke to originally do I ask, "How does this passage relate to my situation or to the situations of other people I know?"

I treated the biblical passages in this book the same way–by including relevant background information before examining the life application for the depressed person.

I did so for two reasons:

First, I believe with the writer of 2 Timothy that all Scripture is inspired by God and is useful for teaching, for reproof, for correction, and for training in righteousness (3:16). If we believe that the Bible contains God's revelation to us, we have an obligation to read and study it for that sake alone, even if certain parts of it do not seem to apply to our current life situation.

Second, when we look at the Bible objectively, we have already made a small step toward overcoming our depression. Depression incarcerates us with subjectivity. *Our* problems, *our* feelings, *our* life situations seem to close in on us, binding us so that we cannot move. When we can look at the world more objectively, we leave that prison for a moment.

When David grieved for Saul and Jonathan, he did not think, "I'm going to write a poem that will help Kathleen deal with her loss and grief three thousand years from now." The lament in 2 Samuel 1:17-27 expresses David's grief alone, and we need to respect its personal nature.

However, we can say, "I can identify with David's feelings a little bit. When my brother died, I was both very angry and very sad. I wonder if writing the lament helped David to feel a little better? I wonder if writing about my loss would help me to feel better?"

Questions for reflection are part of each devotion. Again, I hope that they will serve to help you look at your depression more objectively. If you keep a journal, I would encourage you to write down answers to these questions. If you suffer a recurring episode of depression in the future, they may serve as a road map to help you find your way out.

A short prayer ends each devotion. At times, I have found it helpful to repeat short prayers over and over again as I struggle with difficult issues. During times of anxiety, I often find myself repeating a quote I paraphrased from Henri Nouwen: "The worst thing that can happen has already happened. Jesus Christ was crucified" (*A Cry for Mercy*, Doubleday, 1981, p. 93). The simple act of saying these words has sometimes helped to relieve my pain and anxiety. For many generations, people have found comfort in repeating the words "The Lord is my shepherd, I shall not want." You may wish to create your own repeated prayer as you seek to focus your attention away from your misery.

• • •

As I said before, I have had three episodes of major depression since I was twelve. In that statement is hope, for it means that I have also recovered from three episodes of depression. The probability is great that you also will recover from the despair you feel at this time.

I believe that God works through our depressions to help us grow. As a result of my experiences with it I have become less judgmental, less self-righteous, and more able to empathize with others in their emotional and spiritual struggles. Jesus spent forty days in the wilderness before he began his ministry. I believe that the time we spend in our own spiritual wilderness prepares us to be better servants of God's kingdom.

1

Feeling abandoned

Genesis 21:14-20

So Abraham rose early in the morning, and took bread and a skin of water, and gave it to Hagar, putting it on her shoulder, along with the child, and sent her away. And she departed, and wandered about in the wilderness of Beer-sheba. When the water in the skin was gone, she cast the child under one of the bushes. Then she went and sat down opposite him a good way off, about the distance of a bowshot; for she said, "Do not let me look on the death of the child." And as she sat opposite him, she lifted up her voice and wept. And God heard the voice of the boy; and the angel of God called to Hagar from heaven, and said to her, "What troubles you, Hagar? Do not be afraid; for God has heard the voice of the boy where he is. Come, lift up the boy and hold him fast with your hand, for I will make a great nation of him." Then God opened her eyes and she saw a well of water. She went, and filled the skin with water, and gave the boy a drink. God was with the boy, and he grew up; he lived in the wilderness, and became an expert with the bow.

The ancient Hebrews did not believe in an afterlife—at least not in the same sense that Christians do. One's immortality lived on in one's descendants. Therefore Abraham's and Sarah's childlessness had implications beyond the simple desire of parents to have children for whom they can care.

Childlessness had economic implications for the ancient Hebrews. Parents counted on their children to take care of them when they grew old. Childlessness had cultural implications. Barren couples were stigmatized. And childlessness had spiritual implications. When Abraham and Sarah died, they would be gone forever because they had no heirs to carry on their memory.

Abraham had a son with Hagar, Sarah's slave. He did this to ensure he would have an heir, despite the fact that the angelic visitors in Genesis 18 had told Abraham and Sarah that God would give them a son. When Sarah bore Isaac, she no longer wanted Hagar and her son Ishmael around. She wanted Isaac to be Abraham's sole heir. In 21:11, we read Abraham's reaction: *The matter was very distressing to Abraham on account of his son.* The narrative does not say whether he felt any compassion for the abandoned Hagar.

The story of Hagar and Ishmael is an **etiology.** Etiologies offer explanations of how things came to be as they are. For example, the story of Abraham offering Isaac as a sacrifice and God's miraculous intervention served as an etiology for why the Israelites did not sacrifice their children in religious rituals as some of the neighboring Canaanite tribes did.

The story in Genesis 18 of Abraham, Sarah, Hagar, and Ishmael (along with the parallel account in Genesis 16) is an etiology for why the

Bedouin tribespeople known as the Ishmaelites had so many cultural and linguistic attributes in common with the Israelites. It may have also explained why the Israelites and the Ishmaelites fought with one another. The story could have been told by the Israelites to show that the Ishmaelites, who claimed Abraham as a common ancestor, were of inferior lineage. Hagar was, after all, only a slave. Sarah was Abraham's real wife, and their son was, therefore, more of a real descendant of Abraham.

The story has a theological message apart from its ancient origins. Basically, this message says that when people try to do things apart from God's will, disaster will inevitably result. God had promised Abraham early on that he would have many descendants. Because of their impatience for children, Abraham and Sarah tried to bring this about by arranging for Hagar's impregnation (see Genesis 16).

What was the result? Hagar and her child are driven into the desert, abandoned to a situation which, without God's intervention, would have meant certain death for both of them. We can no longer feel completely at ease with Abraham and Sarah, knowing as we do their failure of compassion. Yet we can feel secure that God will work on behalf of the abandoned and the outcast.

Application

The story of Hagar touches several chords of anguish within us. This slave woman had been treated by her owners as a brood animal. Did she have an opportunity to consent or to refuse

Abraham's sexual attentions? We don't know. The thoughts of slaves are under-represented in history. For submitting and bearing a child for Abraham and Sarah, what did she get? Abandonment in the desert.

When depression lingers for any length of time, we can easily feel abandoned by those we care about and by God. We may count on people to look after us and to protect us. We may do things which we find humiliating in order to ensure some measure of human attention. Where does it get us?

Worse yet is the feeling that God has abandoned us. We have done everything right, we protest. We have prayed and fasted, we have served others, and we had our daily quiet time. So why do we feel so alone?

We need to remember the end of the story. God did not forget Hagar and her child. He gave them water in the desert, which they needed for survival. He assured Hagar that her son would not be just Abraham and Sarah's castoff. He, too, had a destiny. He, too, would live on in his descendants. God will have compassion on us as well.

The other message to remember from this story is that we dare not interfere in God's plan. Sometimes we just need to wait for God's promises to manifest themselves. After we have done all the right things, sometimes we need to stop doing and start being. God will not forget us in our misery. Just as Sarah had a baby when she was long past child-bearing age, so will our misery end some day. But we may have to wait; it may be long after we thought we couldn't stand feeling this way for one more day.

Things to Think About

Can you think of some times in your life when you humiliated yourself in order to retain some person's good opinion of you or to seek someone's attention? What are some people or things that enslave us, things make us feel that we are not in control of our actions or behaviors? Are we actually slaves to these things, or do we just feel like we are? How do we win our freedom?

Who are the people in our society who are really enslaved?

Can you think of some times when you couldn't wait any longer for a situation to change and tried to force a change?

What are the times you feel most alone? Who are the people who have abandoned you? Have you ever abandoned someone who needed you?

Prayer

God, I do not believe you have abandoned me, that you have brought me this far only to leave me. Help me to wait for you to come to me. Help me to reach out to others who feel abandoned. Amen.

2

Dealing with past hurts

Genesis 37:31-35

Then they took Joseph's robe, slaughtered a goat, and dipped the robe in the blood. They had the long robe with sleeves taken to their father, and they said, "This we have found; see now whether it is your son's robe or not." He recognized it, and said, "It is my son's robe! A wild animal has devoured him; Joseph is without doubt torn to pieces." Then Jacob tore his garments, and put sackcloth on his loins, and mourned for his son many days. All his sons and all his daughters sought to comfort him; but he refused to be comforted, and said, "No, I shall go down to Sheol to my son, mourning." Thus his father bewailed him.

When people talk about family values as found in Scripture, we might very well ask, "Whose values?" Those of Abraham, who passed off his wife as his sister and married her to a petty tyrant he feared? Those of Lot, who offered his daughters to the men of Sodom who were intent on raping Lot's guests? Who, in fact, committed incest with his daughters while in a drunken stupor? Those of Jacob and Rebekah, whose blatant favoritism caused their sons, Jacob and Esau, to hate each other? What about the immorality of the Corinthian Christians?

Genesis 37 tells the tragic story of a dysfunctional family. Jacob had always loved Joseph best because he loved Joseph's mother best. In the story of Jacob's reunification with Esau, we read that when Jacob saw Esau coming with four hundred men, he put his concubines and their children in front, then Leah and her children, and finally Rachel and Joseph behind all of them. In the event of an attack by Esau, the children he valued least and their mothers would bear the brunt of it.

In Sunday school we tend to view Joseph's brothers as unscrupulous schemers. But we need to remember that they spent their lives in Joseph's shadow. Jacob unapologetically favored Joseph. His brothers' jealousy ran deep. It wasn't just that Joseph got a coat from their father and they didn't. The gift had great significance. People who wore long coats with long sleeves could not do the dirty work of tending fields and farms. In giving Joseph this gift, Jacob indicated that he was to be the aristocrat of the family. His brothers would perform the hard manual labor.

Small wonder they hated Joseph. Perhaps after selling him into slavery, they had the added satisfaction of knowing that he would finally know what it was like to do some hard work.

Because Jacob had vested all his hopes and all his love in Joseph, he became truly desolate when he lost Joseph. Had he valued his other children more, perhaps their comfort would have meant something to him as he mourned for Joseph. As it was, he would go down to Sheol—the place of insignificant afterlife entirely separated from God—still wearing his sackcloth, so Joseph would know how much his father had mourned him.

One of the most unappreciated virtues of the Bible is its honesty in portraying heroes and followers of the faith as human beings instead of mythical, godlike beings. David, an adulterer and murderer, became the greatest king of Israel. Jesus chose Peter, a coward, to serve as the rock upon which he built his church. Acknowledging the human failings of biblical heroes should serve as a source of comfort rather than a threat to our ideals. If God chose to work through men and women such as these, God can surely work through people such as ourselves. If God can work through dysfunctional families such as Jacob's, God can work through our families as well.

Despite the tragic family situation of Joseph and his brothers, God continued to work within the family and helped to heal it. Joseph and his brothers found each other again in Egypt and perhaps began to act as brothers for the first time. Joseph's family was saved from starvation when he brought his family to Egypt to live with him.

Application

The term *dysfunctional family* has become almost trite. People are questioning the profusion of twelve-step programs and other recovery movements. Witness Wendy Kaminer's book, *I'm Dysfunctional, You're Dysfunctional*, or the Stuart Smalley character on *Saturday Night Live* (I'm good enough, I'm smart enough, and doggone it, people like me!).

The danger of such a backlash is that it discounts millions of people who have experienced varying degrees of trauma as part of their upbringing. Many, perhaps most, people struggling with depression have to go back and sift through these traumas before they can really begin to heal or feel better about themselves.

Maybe your father raped you. Maybe your mother routinely humiliated you. Maybe you regret that you were not as close to your parents as you would have liked. All three examples are valid sources of pain. Some cause less damage and therefore are more easily worked through in therapy, formal or informal.

Nevertheless, depression indicates that something is not working, that something stands in the way of your growth and healing. Perhaps you view that something as trivial. Perhaps you think you have no right to feel depressed about the fact, say, that your parents did not intervene when your older sister used to pick on you. You know people who suffered from far greater abuses or endured tragedies such as the death of a family member. And yet, you feel a persistent sadness when you think about your family. No matter how much you tell yourself that you should feel fortunate for your family situation not having been worse, you still feel sad.

Just because the great majority of families have some sort of dysfunction or another, it does not mean that people should not deal with these dysfunctions. If something has hurt you, no matter how trivial you think the hurt, deal with it. That small hurt may be what stands in the way of your feeling whole again.

Things to think about

If you could change any aspect of your upbringing, what would you change?

List the ten most damaging things you think could happen to a child. Which of them happened to you? What did you do at the time it happened? Is there anything you can do about it now?

Wendy Kaminer speaks of the "cult of victimization." What do you think she means by that? How have you been victimized? How have you victimized others?

Have you ever felt that your parents or other adults in your life valued other children more than they valued you? Do you have favorites among your siblings or children?

How would you have to change in order for there to be healing in your family? How would the other members of your family have to change?

Prayer

Lord, thank you for working through our failures as families and as individuals. Give me the courage to face my past and the strength to move beyond it. Amen.

3

Facing feelings of loss

2 Samuel 3:12-16

Abner sent messengers to David at Hebron, saying, "To whom does the land belong? Make your covenant with me, and I will give you my support to bring all Israel over to you." He said, "Good; I will make a covenant with you. But one thing I require of you: you shall never appear in my presence unless you bring Saul's daughter Michal when you come to see me." Then David sent messengers to Saul's son Ishbaal, saying, "Give me my wife Michal, to whom I became engaged at the price of one hundred foreskins of the Philistines." Ishbaal sent and took her from her husband Paltiel the son of Laish. But her husband went with her, weeping as he walked behind her all the way to Bahurim. Then Abner said to him, "Go back home!" So he went back.

Saul's daughter Michal loved David. But instead of blessing this relationship, Saul used it as an opportunity to rid himself of David. In exchange for his daughter Michal, Saul required that David kill one hundred Philistines (and bring him their foreskins as proof). When the Philistines did not kill David, as Saul had hoped, Saul kept his promise and let Michal marry David. Not giving up, Saul decided to take a more direct approach in arranging for David's murder. Michal found out about it and helped David to escape, and he fled the court. Later, Saul married Michal to Paltiel (called "Palti" in 1 Samuel 25:44), son of Laish.

Paltiel is not a name that springs to mind when one thinks of significant figures in the Bible. That was his problem. In the war between David and Saul, he was an insignificant character. The fact that he loved his wife meant nothing in comparison to the political maneuverings of these great war heroes. What did his brother-in-law Ishbaal say to Paltiel when he told him that Michal must be returned to David? Did he say that David had paid for her and thus his property must be returned to him?

The passage for today does not say what Michal felt when told she must leave Paltiel. One can only conjecture what it was like to leave a man who loved her deeply and become one of several wives and concubines in David's court. We can imagine also what it was like to return to a man at war with the rest of her family.

The only record of her relationship with David after this time appears in 2 Samuel 6:16-23 (see also 1 Chronicles 15:29). When the ark of the Lord returned to Jerusalem, David danced about, nearly naked, in joy and triumph. When Michal saw this, she "despised him in her heart."

Application

Losing someone we love through rejection or death is probably the deepest emotional pain human beings suffer. The loss has such force because we can do nothing to prevent it. However hard we try, we cannot make someone love us. We cannot stop death from eventually taking away everyone we care about.

Sometimes it amazes us that the world keeps revolving, oblivious to our loss. Politics and wars, school and postal deliveries carry on over the din of grief and anguish screaming inside us.

We lack control over many things besides love and death, of course. One of the most debilitating effects of depression is the lack of control we have over how we feel. We know that we ought to feel differently. We purposely set out to do things that will serve as an antidote to our depression. Perhaps we sing songs that comforted us in the past, read books, visit with friends. These things may offer a brief respite, but eventually we return to the gloom that has become the norm for us.

We realize that our depression does not really matter much in the big scheme of things. In fact, we may feel disgusted with ourselves for being so self-absorbed while famines, wars, and other gross injustices run rampant in the rest of the world. This disgust, in turn, puts us on a downward spiral that, again, we seem unable to control.

What comfort can we take from the story of Paltiel and Michal?

We need to remember that even though their feelings meant little to Saul or David, they meant something to God. To paraphrase Jesus, if God worries about the fall of one sparrow, then surely God feels the anguish of a husband who has become separated from his wife through forces beyond his control. God surely feels our own losses more keenly than we do.

God, infinite in power, can identify with us when we feel powerless. Jesus knew what helplessness felt like as he sought God's will for his life and death.

Things to Think About

What are some situations in your life that you feel are out of your control? Are there aspects of this situation that you can control (for example, removing yourself from the situation)?

Have you ever felt you were a pawn in someone else's strategy?

Do you believe that God cares about your problems?

Which events, either global or local, seem larger than your own pain? Which events seem insignificant when placed beside your own pain?

Prayer

God, I believe that you share in my feelings of loss and powerlessness. I believe that you feel them even more deeply than I do, and I believe that you will help me bear them. Amen.

4

Letting go of the past

2 Samuel 18:31—19:1-7

Then the Cushite came; and the Cushite said, "Good tidings for my lord the king! For the LORD has vindicated you this day, delivering you from the power of all who rose up against you." The king said to the Cushite, "Is it well with the young man Absalom?" The Cushite answered, "May the enemies of my lord the king, and all who rise up to do you harm, be like that young man." The king was deeply moved, and went up to the chamber over the gate, and wept; and as he went, he said, "O my son Absalom, my son, my son Absalom! Would I had died instead of you, O Absalom, my son, my son!" It was told Joab, "The king is weeping and mourning for Absalom." So the victory that day was turned into mourning for all the troops; for the troops heard that day, "The king is grieving for his son." The troops stole into the city that day as soldiers steal in who are ashamed when they flee in battle. The king covered his face, and the king cried with a loud voice, "O my son Absalom, O Absalom, my son, my son!" Then Joab came into the house to the king, and said, "Today you have covered with shame the faces of all your officers who have saved your life today, and the lives of your sons and your daughters, and the lives of your wives and your concubines, for love of those who hate you and for hatred of those who love you. You have made it clear today that commanders and officers are nothing to you; for I perceive that if Absalom were alive and all of us were dead today, then you would be pleased. So go out at once and speak kindly to your servants; for I swear by the LORD, if you do not go, not a man will stay with you this night; and this will be worse for you than any disaster that has come upon you from your youth until now."

It all began when David's son Amnon raped David's daughter Tamar. We read in 2 Samuel 13:21, "When King David heard of all these things, he became very angry, but he would not punish his son Amnon, because he loved him, for he was his firstborn." Absalom, Tamar's brother and Amnon's half-brother, subsequently murdered Amnon two years later and fled for his life.

Ultimately, Absalom and his father found themselves at war with each other. David fled from the city, and Absalom usurped the throne in Jerusalem. David's and Absalom's armies met in the forest of Ephraim, and many lives were lost. While riding through the forest, Absalom's head became caught in an oak tree and he was left hanging. Joab, David's officer, thrust three spears into him while he hung there.

Joab and his men had restored David to his throne. The rebellion was over. David, however, felt no relief or joy in his victory. His son, Absalom, whom he loved, was dead.

What would have happened if David had punished Amnon for raping Tamar? Would Absalom have sought power had he felt David had administered power justly? It is possible, of course, that Absalom might have killed Amnon merely because he knew he was in line for the throne. However, if David had taken a little more interest in his children, if he hadn't shown Amnon so much favor, would he have had cause to grieve at the violent death of yet another son?

Personal greatness in the Bible does not always translate into parenting skills. Think of Samuel's sons, whom the Israelites did not trust to follow in the footsteps of their father. Think of the prophet Isaiah, who named his sons The Spoil Speeds, The Prey Hastens, and A Remnant Will Return. Think of how the children in the neighborhood must have tormented these boys!

As with the story of Jacob and his sons, however, the story of David and his children teaches that God works through weak and sinful human beings. David was a weak parent, but he was also a great leader who kept his people from falling into the sin of idolatry–a problem that would plague the successors to his throne.

In the story today, we see David confronted by the outcome of his failures as a parent. His awareness of this failure must have greatly magnified the anguish he felt over his son's death. Joab, his army officer, reprimanded him sharply. Thousands of people had put their lives on the line for David. He had a great many children who had not rebelled but had supported him. Joab told David it was impermissible for him to turn away from the people who had supported him to indulge himself in a private grief for a son who had betrayed him. David heeded his words and went out to sit in the gate of the city. His troops rallied around him.

Application

We cannot change the past. However, the phrase "No use crying over spilt milk" does not really address the difficulty faced in letting go of the past any more than someone telling us to cheer up addresses the difficulty of living with depression.

People rarely make a clean break with the traumas of their past. Some people think they have when they have only encased it with a denial stronger and heavier than any type of mortar. "I've put all that behind me," they might say. "Once I gave my life to Jesus, all the bad stuff that happened in my family didn't control me anymore."

Yet these people continue to drag the burdens of the past with them, pretending not see them, until the new burdens of their present life tip the balance and everything comes crashing down.

It is healthier by far to face the past, to say, "When my father did this to me, it hurt me and I have never gotten over it."

There comes a point, however, when dissection of the past becomes wallowing in self-pity. The line between the two is very fine. Just as it is a mistake to avoid dealing with the past by saying "Oh my, I've just got to stop wallowing in self-pity," so is it a mistake to say "I refuse to let go of the past until everything is completely resolved."

We can never completely resolve the hurts of our past. We can ask forgiveness from the people we have hurt and grant forgiveness to the people who have hurt us. Rarely can we forget that the hurts have occurred. Like David, however, we need to let go of these hurts so that we can get on with the business of living. God can free us–not from our memories but from the emotional baggage that immobilizes us.

Things to Think About

Have you ever neglected the supportive people in your life in your preoccupation with people who have hurt you?

Who are the people in your past you have forgiven? Who are the people you haven't forgiven?

What are the traumas of your past? If you would find it helpful, make a list of the five worst things that ever happened to you. How did you respond at the time they happened? How do you respond to each of these today? Which traumas do you feel you have worked through? Which traumas still have some control over your emotional life?

Why is it hard for you to let go of things that happened to you in the past? What would help you most to let go?

Prayer

God, help me to face my past without self-pity. Give me the wisdom to know the right time to let go of the things that have hurt me. Amen.

5

Healing as a gift from God

2 Kings 5:9-15

So Naaman came with his horses and chariots, and halted at the entrance of Elisha's house. Elisha sent a messenger to him, saying, "Go, wash in the Jordan seven times, and your flesh shall be restored and you shall be clean." But Naaman became angry and went away, saying, "I thought that for me he would surely come out, and stand and call on the name of the LORD his God, and would wave his hand over the spot, and cure the leprosy! Are not Abana and Pharpar, the rivers of Damascus, better than all the waters of Israel? Could I not wash in them, and be clean?" He turned and went away in a rage. But his servants approached and said to him, "Father, if the prophet had commanded you to do something difficult, would you not have done it? How much more, when all he said to you was, 'Wash, and be clean'?" So he went down and immersed himself seven times in the Jordan, according to the word of the man of God; his flesh was restored like the flesh of a young boy, and he was clean. Then he returned to the man of God, he and all his company; he came and stood before him and said, "Now I know that there is no God in all the earth except in Israel; please accept a present from your servant."

Naaman commanded the army of the King of Aram (roughly the area we call Syria today), and he had leprosy. A slave girl captured by the Arameans in one of their raids in Israel told Naaman's wife that there was a prophet in Israel who would heal Naaman's illness. Accordingly, the king of Aram commanded the king of Israel to see to it that Naaman would get healed. The king of Israel thought that the king of Aram was looking for an excuse to make war with him and plunder Israel.

He did not think about the prophet Elisha who lived within his kingdom. Elijah and Elisha were never on the best of terms with the kings of Israel. Elisha, however, took the matter in hand and told the king to send Naaman to him, so, he added wryly, "that he may learn that there is a prophet in Israel."

In this passage we see that Elisha did not even bother to come out when Naaman arrived. He sent a messenger to tell Naaman to bathe in the Jordan seven times. To appreciate Naaman's reaction to this message, we need to consider that at places during the dry season, the Jordan River is little more than a muddy creek. To have traveled all the way from Aram and then be told to go wash in the creek was an insult to a man as proud and powerful as Naaman. He had expected better, perhaps a miraculous healing through the wave of a hand. At least he must have expected Elisha to come out and say hello!

Fortunately, Naaman had sensible servants. If Elisha had told him to slaughter several oxen and parade around them blowing a horn seventy times while priests muttered incantations, Naaman probably would have gone along with it. Elisha had suggested something a lot less troublesome. It wouldn't hurt to try doing as he asked, suggested the servants.

He followed the instructions and his leprosy went away. Elisha had demonstrated his standing as a prophet. Naaman converted and became a follower of the one God, and possibly the kingdom of Israel was saved from a war with the the kingdom of Aram.

The story of Naaman offers some insight into the character of Elisha and into the historical view that the Israelites had of their prophets. Prophets did not ordinarily show a great degree of courtesy or deference to great people. They were not members of the political or religious establishments. Their function was to speak for God. In the case of Elijah and Elisha, they demonstrated the power of God through performing miracles.

In thinking of the continuity between Elijah, Elisha, and the later prophets, one connecting thread lies in the prophets' assertion that God does not expect grand and complicated acts of worship on the part of the people. All Naaman had to do to receive healing from God was to follow Elisha's instructions, as simple or ridiculous as they sounded.

This simplicity of obedience can also be found in the prophecy of Micah, who told the people, "He has told you, O mortal, what is good; and what does the Lord require of you but to do justice, and to love kindness, and to walk humbly with your God (Micah 6:8)?

Application

Sometimes the suggestions professionals give us do not make sense when we first try to address our depression through psychological or medical therapy. Why should we allow ourselves to feel anger? We're better Christians than that. The people who have rejected us or whom we have alienated won't want to be with us if we get angry.

And how are pills supposed to make this misery go away? We have reasons for feeling depressed about all the stresses in our lives. Taking pills will not make these stresses go away.

Christianity and psychiatry have not yet become comfortable bedfellows. Our religion helps us to define the reasons that have brought us to a spiritual crisis. Our doctors have researched the psychological and medical roots of the same crisis. The cures that each suggests might be ridiculed by the other. To take time for prayer and spiritual retreat does not appear in most psychiatrists' written recommendations. To prescribe a course of medication that will rectify chemical imbalances does not come within the the domain of the pastor.

Most of us have no objection to seeing a doctor for cancer, broken bones, or headaches. We believe that God's healing power can come through in the attention of our doctors. We should not doubt that God can also work through the attention of psychiatrists and psychotherapists. If medication can help to heal our depression, why not take so simple a route? We would not begrudge ourselves crutches while we waited for our broken leg to heal.

Things to Think About

When you hear words such as "psychiatrist" or "psychotherapist," what are the first images that come to your mind? How do psychiatrists differ in your mind from other medical doctors?

Can you think of a time when a solution to a problem was much simpler than you thought it would be? What are some spiritual avenues you have found useful in the past for healing during stressful times?

Prayer

God, help me to accept your healing in all forms. Help me to see simple solutions to my problems rather than designing complicated ones of my own. Amen.

6

Acknowledging the world as it is

2 Kings 6:24-31

Some time later King Ben-hadad of Aram mustered his entire army; he marched against Samaria and laid siege to it. As the siege continued, famine in Samaria became so great that a donkey's head was sold for eighty shekels of silver, and one-fourth of a kab of dove's dung for five shekels of silver. Now as the king of Israel was walking on the city wall, a woman cried out to him, "Help, my lord king!" He said, "No! Let the LORD help you. How can I help you? From the threshing floor or from the wine press?" But then the king asked her, "What is your complaint?" She answered, "This woman said to me, 'Give up your son; we will eat him today, and we will eat my son tomorrow.' So we cooked my son and ate him. The next day I said to her, 'Give up your son and we will eat him.' But she has hidden her son." When the king heard the words of the woman he tore his clothes—now since he was walking on the city wall, the people could see that he had sackcloth on his body underneath—and he said, "So may God do to me, and more, if the head of Elisha son of Shaphat stays on his shoulders today."

This passage surely ranks among the most disturbing in the entire Bible. In 2 Kings 5 we learned of the superior military power that the Arameans had over the Israelites. In 2 Kings 6 we see the results of their siege warfare against the city of Samaria. Siege warfare was common because most cities of any size were contained within a city wall in the Ancient Near East. (See 2 Kings 18:13–19:1-37 or Isaiah 36–37 for accounts of the Assyrian's siege of Jerusalem.)

The advantage in this type of warfare was always with the armies laying the siege. If they waited patiently, starvation would ultimately force the hand of the people within the city wall. This is the case in the above passage. According to the *New Oxford Annotated Bible*, eighty shekels would have equaled a British pound, and that was the price for a worthless part of an unkosher animal. A kab would have equaled about a quart.

It would be far better, however, to subsist on doves' dung than to take the course of the two women in this passage. The king reacted to the horror of the situation in an entirely appropriate manner. He had been wearing sackcloth, which denoted mourning and repentance, during the course of the siege. He did not parade around ostentatiously showing his repentance, but his people could not help but see the sackcloth when he ripped his robes in grief and fury.

The only inappropriate response on the king's part was to blame Elisha for the sore straits to which the city had been reduced. Perhaps Elisha had advised the king to hold out against the

Arameans. Perhaps, because he prophesied a time of famine, the king held him in some way responsible (see 2 Kings 8:1).

Perhaps, like a child, he just wanted Elisha to make everything all better. In the story immediately preceding this one in 2 Kings 6:8-23, Elisha and the king were on good terms. Elisha had captured the Aramean army through divine intervention, and the king deferred to Elisha in deciding what to do with the captured men. If Elisha could call on that sort of power, perhaps the king wondered why he didn't do so at this time. Couldn't he see how exceedingly desperate the situation in Samaria was?

The horror of today's passage has repeated itself many times in history. Perhaps the most recent memory of children being cannibalized was when Stalin imposed mass starvation on the people of the Ukraine. In every age when horrors such as this occur, people have asked, "Why didn't God do something to make it better? Couldn't God see the enormity of the suffering? Has God no compassion at all?"

Application

When people struggle with depression, one of their coping devices is to put things into perspective. They imagine how much worse off they could feel if they found themselves in the middle of one of the current global catastrophes.

There is a time and place for saying, "In light of the situation in ______ (Bosnia, Somalia, Haiti, etc.), I guess this thing I'm struggling with is not such a big deal." However, when one is in the deepest throes of depression, comparing one's own situation to others in more desperate situations can be counterproductive. Reflecting on the experiences of people suffering famine, war, or the death of a loved one can produce the thought, "I'm just barely getting by now, coping with comparatively minor stresses. If I had to face what those people are facing, I really would kill myself."

How then do we respond to the great tragedies we read about or see on the news? Should we become isolationist and not expose ourselves to information that will only depress us more? Perhaps, for some people at some times, this route might be best. We cannot help anyone else if we find ourselves completely immobilized with our own depression.

Eventually, however, we need to accept the world as it is. There is a lot of horror and sadness in the world. As creatures fallen from grace, human beings will inevitably cause tremendous suffering.

The trick is to find ways, however small, in which we can reflect the grace of God. Maybe we cannot prevent wars or avert famines or even control our moods. But we can choose to treat those closest to us kindly. We can find out who the people are who are working to promote peace and justice in their communities and around the world. We can offer them our support through prayer or perhaps through our financial resources.

Helping others is not the surefire way of curing depression that some people say it is. But it can help bring us out of ourselves for a short time. It can help us feel that we accomplished one good thing in a day otherwise overwhelmed by personal stresses.

Helping others also helps us to demonstrate a hope that we may not feel. In serving others because we believe it is what God wants, we indicate that we believe God reigns. It demonstrates a faith that Christ will come again and establish a kingdom untouched by the horrors of our world.

Things to Think About

What stresses in your life do you find most overwhelming? What current events around the world do you find most overwhelming?

When confronted by a desperate situation, do you feel a desire to confront it or to withdraw from it?

What are some practical ways in which you help others build the kingdom of God? What are some practical ways you have observed others doing kingdom building?

What is the very worst thing that could possibly happen? How does belief in God make a difference?

Prayer

God, I believe you are greater than the greatest tragedy in the world today. Grant me strength to face the horrors and do what I can to make a difference. Amen.

7

Cautious trusting

Nehemiah 2:1-5

In the month of Nisan, in the twentieth year of King Artaxerxes, when wine was served him, I carried the wine and gave it to the king. Now, I had never been sad in his presence before. So the king said to me, "Why is your face sad, since you are not sick? This can only be sadness of the heart." Then I was very much afraid. I said to the king, "May the king live forever! Why should my face not be sad, when the city, the place of my ancestors' graves, lies waste, and its gates have been destroyed by fire?" Then the king said to me, "What do you request?" So I prayed to the God of heaven. Then I said to the king, "If it pleases the king, and if your servant has found favor with you, I ask that you send me to Judah, to the city of my ancestors' graves, so that I may rebuild it."

In 539 B.C.E., King Cyrus of Persia captured Babylon, the capitol city of the Babylonian empire. Both Babylonian and Persian historical records report that the inhabitants of Babylon welcomed the conquerors because they resented the rule of the Babylonian king, Nabonidus, especially the religious innovations he sought to impose on his people.

The Jews, whom Nebuchadnezzar had first deported to Babylon in 597 B.C.E., had a special reason to hope for good things to come. We find some of this hope expressed in the book of Isaiah:

> [W]ho says of Cyrus, "He is my shepherd, and he shall carry out all my purpose"; and who says of Jerusalem, "It shall be rebuilt," and of the temple, "Your foundation shall be laid" (Isaiah 44:28).

> Thus says the LORD to his anointed, to Cyrus, whose right hand I have grasped to subdue nations before him and strip kings of their robes, to open doors before him–and the gates shall not be closed (Isaiah 45:1).

> I have aroused Cyrus in righteousness, and I will make all his paths straight; he shall build my city and set my exiles free, not for price or reward, says the LORD of hosts (Isaiah 45:13).

Cyrus did not disappoint the Jews. In his famous edict of 538 B.C.E., he said that they could return to their homeland. Furthermore, he ordered the temple in Jerusalem rebuilt at the expense of the royal treasury. And he decreed that all the sacred vessels that the Babylonians had plundered should be returned to Jerusalem.

Some might argue that Cyrus showed more political astuteness than generosity in concerning himself with a relatively unimportant people such as the Jews. It was certainly to his advantage to have loyal and grateful subjects in Palestine, serving as it did as a bridge to Egypt. But, in fact, benevolence characterized the reign of the Persians.

We see some of this spirit in the passage for

today. Artaxerxes, fifth in line from Cyrus, had a massive kingdom to run. He had to deal with rebellions in Egypt and Syria and face the encroaching threat of the Greek Empire. Yet he took the time to take notice of his servant Nehemiah's troubled spirit. The word translated as "sad" is more usually translated as "bad," "disagreeable," or "evil." Nehemiah had reason to feel afraid. An intimate servant of the king should always present a pleasing outward appearance, after all. He knew he should not have let his inner despair over news from Jerusalem affect his work.

Yet Artaxerxes did not reprimand Nehemiah. He wanted to know what troubled him.

What Nehemiah really wanted was to go to Judea and organize the people there to rebuild Jerusalem. Nearly a hundred years after the Edict of Cyrus, Jerusalem still lay in ruins. The exiles who had trickled back to Judah over this period of time met with great hostility from their neighbors Samaria and Edom. When the Jews attempted to rebuild the wall around Jerusalem, officials of Samaria told Artaxerxes that the Jews did so out of disloyalty to him. Artaxerxes thus ordered the construction of the wall stopped.

Nehemiah mentioned his ancestors' graves before referring to the rest of Jerusalem. The king was in the process of constructing his own royal tomb at the time, and Nehemiah may have seen a way to enlist the king's sympathy. Evidently, he succeeded in doing so, for Artaxerxes reversed his previous order. In Nehemiah 2:8 we read, "And the king granted me what I asked, for the gracious hand of my God was upon me."

Application

What does this excursion into fifth-century Middle Eastern politics have to do with you?

Just as Nehemiah showed caution in approaching the king regarding his distress, so do we show caution in approaching others about our depression. There are certain safe people we can approach, such as therapists and pastors, but who else can we share our anguish with? Sometimes family members and close friends are precisely the people we cannot open up to. To tell someone who cares about us that we find our lives unbearable is to place a great burden on that person. Even though the people who care about us may gladly shoulder that burden, it is not something we undertake to give them lightly.

We also need to show caution in sharing our depression with people who do not have our interests at heart. In the 1972 U.S. presidential election, the press found out that George McGovern's running mate, Thomas Eagleton, had received psychiatric treatment for depression. McGovern subsequently dropped Eagleton and chose Sargent Shriver as a vice-presidential candidate.

When Michael Dukakis ran against George Bush in 1988, rumors began to spread that he too had been treated for depression. Dukakis adamantly denied it. Millions of depressed Americans thus had their fears confirmed that seeking help for their depression rendered their competence suspect.

Perhaps the day will come when we will no longer have to be careful about referring to our depression. For now, it is important that we have at least one or two people to whom we can speak openly about it. Knowing the right people and the right time to share our disability calls for shrewd judgment.

Things to Think About

Who are the people in your life that you trust implicitly? Have you shared with them the realities of your depression? Why or why not?

Has speaking to someone about your depression ever had negative consequences? How did you respond? How did the experience change your inclination to speak about your depression?

What is the worst thing that could happen if you shared information about your depression with someone?

Have you ever known people who were too open about discussing their depression? Can a person become a hypochondriac in the area of mental health? Have you ever felt that you talked too much about your condition to other people?

Prayer

God, grant me the wisdom to know to whom I can turn in my distress. Create in me an instinct to turn to you first. Amen.

8

Be present in my pain

Job 2:11-13

Now when Job's three friends heard of all these troubles that had come upon him, each of them set out from his home—Eliphaz the Temanite, Bildad the Shuhite, and Zophar the Naamathite. They met together to go and console and comfort him. When they saw him from a distance, they did not recognize him, and they raised their voices and wept aloud; they tore their robes and threw dust in the air upon their heads. They sat with him on the ground seven days and seven nights, and no one spoke a word to him, for they saw that his suffering was very great.

People often remember Job's friends as nosy busybodies, intent on blaming Job for his own misfortune. However, this passage shows them in another light. They did not come to judge Job at all. They came to console and comfort him. As long as Job sat among the ashes of the garbage dump outside of the town, mute in his woe, the friends said nothing. They sat and shared in his suffering and mourning.

Indeed, it was not until Job spoke—until he asked "Why?" in verses 11, 12, 20, and 23—that his friend Eliphaz tried to answer his question.

Each of Job's friends in turn tried to convince him that he had erred in some way, that he had somehow deserved the fate he was suffering. If Job had not spoken or asked "Why?" would they have done so? Or would they have continued to sit and grieve with him?

Application

When we see people we love suffering, we want to help them. We want to say the right thing. We stand awkwardly, waiting for something to come out of our mouths that will alleviate their pain. That something rarely comes.

This realization can help us when friends or family say exactly the wrong thing to help us out of our depression. They mean well when they say, "You've got to count your blessings. Think of how many people are worse off than you," or "When I feel down like that, I just praise the Lord (or read a Psalm, etc.) and the Lord takes the burden from my heart," or "If you would just get right with God, you wouldn't need to take that medication."

Sometimes the best thing friends can do for us is to be there as Job's friends were, sharing in his mourning. To have someone cook a meal for us, invite us on a walk, or out to a movie can heal in ways that advice cannot. Perhaps when we know that our friends do not have the answers for our depression, we need to refrain from asking them questions that demand a response. We need to let them know, rather, that it is in their presence that we find healing.

I wrote the following poem for some friends who had seen me through a particularly rough period of my life:

Seabirds

When you lit like seabirds on my broken mast,
as I grabbed at flailing ropes with bloody hands
in vain attempts to make the sails fast,
I would have known, but for my desperate fear
that seabirds never travel far from land.
Your presence showed me Land was near.

Things to Think About

What have friends said to you to help when you have been depressed? What did they say that really helped you? What did they say that made it worse?

When have you said the wrong things to people who were suffering?

Whom do you feel you can ask for advice in managing your depression?

Prayer

God, thank you for giving me friends and family who care about me. Help me to accept graciously the help they offer. Help me not to demand answers they are unable to give. Amen.

9

Stronger than we think

Job 6:8-13

"O that I might have my request, and that God would grant my desire; that it would please God to crush me, that he would let loose his hand and cut me off! This would be my consolation; I would even exult in unrelenting pain; for I have not denied the words of the Holy One. What is my strength, that I should wait? And what is my end, that I should be patient? Is my strength the strength of stones, or is my flesh bronze? In truth I have no help in me, and any resource is driven from me."

In Job 3, Job expressed three wishes: (1) that he had never been born, (2) that he had died at birth, (3) that his life might end now. In chapters 4 and 5 his friend Eliphaz endeavored to make some response, countering the cries of anguish with logical discourse. Eliphaz's words offered no comfort to Job, of course, and Job replied bitterly in 6:1-7. His prosperous friend had not the barest idea of Job's suffering. If it were possible to weigh the calamity that had fallen on Job, it would weigh more than "all the sand of the sea." Can't Eliphaz see that it was God who caused Job's tragedy? Job claimed that he had been poisoned by "the arrows of the Almighty."

In verses 8-13, Job returned to the theme begun in verse three. He wanted his misery to end. His belief that God has authored his misery caused him to wish that he might no longer have a relationship with God. If God would only cut Job off, as a tyrannical parent might disinherit a child, then Job would feel free to blaspheme. He could tell God exactly what he thought of this Creator (although he seems to do a reasonably effective job of that anyway).

As it is, he no longer felt strong enough to bear the crushing weight of his misfortune. Because he chose to remain faithful to God, he must bear the misery that God sent him. Job is made of mortal flesh. He feels pain. He wondered, "Does God think that I am made of stone or metal? Why does God continue to heap pain upon overwhelming pain upon me?"

Job concluded by saying that he has nothing left within himself that would enable him to go on. Eliphaz's sermon had driven away any last remnants of his fortitude.

Application

A friend of mine had been in therapy because her husband had fallen in love with another woman. At one point, in despair, she told her counselor that she could just not go on anymore. The situation was too much for her to handle. Her counselor informed her, "You're not a china doll, you know."

Sometimes we feel more fragile than a china doll. Our hearts are already brittle from having been broken daily. We simply cannot face one more hardship, one more jolt of pain.

And yet, the hardships do keep coming, and we do go on. Like Job, we cry out that we are only made of flesh and blood. We are not stone. How can God continue to allow the pain to grind into us?

Also like Job, we are denied a quick end to our sufferings. As followers of God, we do not have the option of suicide. The God who seemingly allows our suffering to hold us will not grant us the right to escape this suffering.

We need to remember that we really are not made of china. We are all stronger than we think we are. Job was stronger than he thought he was, for he did survive–not only his calamities but also his angry confrontations with God.

Things to Think About

What were some times in your life when you felt you could not handle one more calamity? What happened? Did you handle it or were you able to escape?

Have you ever felt that God was responsible for your misery? How did this affect your prayer life?

Do you have an answer to the question of why God allows bad things to happen to people?

Have you ever considered suicide as an option? If yes, do you still consider it an option? What has kept you from killing yourself in the past? How do your responsibilities to God and to other people affect your decisions in this area?

Prayer

God, I do not always feel strong enough to handle

the stresses in my life. Fill me with the knowledge of your strength when I do not feel strong enough to go on. Amen.

10

Waiting for healing

Job 7:1-4

"Do not human beings have a hard service on earth, and are not their days like the days of a laborer? Like a slave who longs for the shadow, and like laborers who look for their wages, so I am allotted months of emptiness, and nights of misery are apportioned to me. When I lie down I say, 'When shall I rise?' But the night is long, and I am full of tossing until dawn."

Hebrew poetry uses a poetic device known as parallelism. A parallelism happens when the writer uses several different words to express an idea in order to intensify the meaning. In the Psalms and the words of the prophets we find many examples of parallelism. Consider this famous example from Isaiah 40:3, "A voice cries out: In the wilderness prepare the way of the Lord. Make straight in the desert a highway for our God.

In Job 7:1-4, the first parallel couplet is, "Do not human beings have hard service on earth" and "are not their days like the days of the laborer?" The couplet might indicate that Job came from an upper-class background because he compared his emotional and physical misery to the toil of a laborer. Job did not envy the situation of others as he emerged a bit from his sorrow to consider the circumstances of others. Instead, as he compared his fate to others, he saw that everyone is miserable for some reason or another.

In the second couplet, "slave who longs for the shadow" and "laborers who look for their wages," Job presented a startling notion of comfort. Note that what the slave and the laborers look forward to are really small benefits. A slave working in the fields under a hot sun would welcome a chance to rest in the shade, but it would not do much to make slavery less burdensome. Peasant laborers might look forward to getting paid so that they might buy food at the end of a long day, but it would not make their lives as landless tenant farmers much easier.

So what are the small comforts Job looked forward to? "months of emptiness" and "nights of misery." Small comforts, indeed. In fact, how could Job consider these comforts at all? What would be the alternative to no longer having to face the passage of time?

The answer is nonexistence. Job preferred the dragging pain of his life to nonexistence. This may seem inconsistent for Job, who several times expressed a wish for his death (e.g., 3:21). However, when looked at from a psychological vantage point, it makes sense.

People with suicidal feelings do not wish to die. They want to be out of pain. If they had some hope that their pain would lessen in the future, they probably would not wish to kill themselves.

Unfortunately no one can predict the future, and depression tends to endow the future with a pessimistic aura.

Job had no hope for the future except his fear of it. His fear of the unknown country he would find himself in after crossing death's boundary was enough to prevent him from killing himself.

Application

Someone once told me, after having undergone some counseling, "I feel stronger now. I find myself more able to cope with the pain, but what I want to know is, Will I have to cope with it forever? Am I going to spend the rest of my life finding coping devices for my depression?"

The stabbing pain of grief hurts far more than the dull ache of depression. But after one has suffered a long depression, grief can look attractive. To feel anything strongly feels preferable to the dragging on of muted pain. Also, grief feels more legitimate than depression in a lot of ways. Grief usually has a more obvious cause, such as the loss of a loved one, whereas depression does not always have an obvious source.

As depression drags on with no end in sight, we need to learn to wait creatively. Learning to wait may seem incongruous when it seems that you have done nothing but wait to feel better. But there is a difference between waiting creatively with faith and waiting in dread of what will come.

I have found it helpful in the past to consider previous episodes of depression and remember what happened around the time they ended. I remember clearly one night going out with friends to a coffeehouse. As I drove home, I realized I had had fun, and that this was the first time I had had fun in over a year and a half. That event helped me through some rough times because I can say to myself, "You know that your depression did end last time. You can remember when it happened. You will see the end of your depression this time, too."

Things to Think About

Do you find that considering the plight of others intensifies your depression or does it help you to put things in perspective?

What are some of the small comforts that make your life more bearable when you are depressed? Do you know why they make you feel better? Do they sometimes make you feel worse afterwards?

Do you consider yourself a patient or impatient person? How can patience and impatience each be used constructively and destructively when you feel depressed?

Think of the last time you had an episode of depression, or ask another person to describe an episode of his or her depression to you. Make a time line for it. Write down events that occurred around the beginning of this depression, during the depression, and at the end of the depression. Now make a second time line, representing your current episode of depression. What events occurred around the time you started feeling depressed? What has happened since it began? Have these events helped your depression or aggravated it? Use a dotted line to represent the future. What events that occurred at the end of the first depression might help you now?

Prayer

God, give me the faith to wait patiently in expectation of healing. I believe that I will not always feel this way. Amen.

11

Using anger creatively

Job 10:1-8

"I loathe my life; I will give free utterance to my complaint; I will speak in the bitterness of my soul. I will say to God, Do not condemn me; let me know why you contend against me. Does it seem good to you to oppress, to despise the work of your hands and favor the schemes of the wicked? Do you have eyes of flesh? Do you see as humans see? Are your days like the days of mortals, or your years like human years, that you seek out my iniquity and search for my sin, although you know that I am not guilty, and there is no one to deliver out of your hand? Your hands fashioned and made me; and now you turn and destroy me."

Whatever criticisms may be made of Job, one cannot accuse him of cowardice or beating around the bush. In the above passage, Job gives a frank assessment of his life and hurls some startling accusations at God.

Job will not hide the extent of his misery for the sake of not offending others. His life had become utterly loathsome to him. God appeared to have condemned him to death by slow torture, and he wants to know why. Does God have a sadistic streak? Did God create Job and develop a loving relationship with him only to discard Job like a used tissue? Did Job have it wrong all along, thinking that God favored righteousness when actually God preferred the wicked?

Job asks if God has mortal characteristics. Scholarly opinion is divided over the intent of this question. Some conclude that Job questioned God's judgment, implying that it is no more inherently just or righteous than any other mortal's judgment. An alternative interpretation is that Job says God deliberately makes unjust choices just as most people do.

Either interpretation is disturbing. We view God as an all-good, all-powerful being. Job at this point seems to utter blasphemy.

And yet, most people at some time in their life become angry with God, because they feel God has betrayed their loyalty. Job, as we learn in chapter 1, was "blameless and upright, one who feared God and turned away from evil." And what became of him? His ten children died horrible deaths and he was reduced to sitting on an ash heap scraping away at skin sores with a shard of pottery. Would a just God have repaid Job's loyalty in such a way? Job comes to the conclusion that a just God would not. Therefore, he concludes, God is not just. Indeed, he asks whether there is not someone who will save him from God's injustice.

Application

Someone I know once told me that she decided one night to get drunk because she was angry at God. She had conscientiously served God from the time she was a teenager, and when she married, she conscientiously tried to be a good wife.

And yet, her husband had several affairs and their marriage fell apart. She had never gotten drunk before, she said, and wanted to do so to "spite God." As she threw up into the toilet, she had a sense of God saying to her, "You're going to have to do a lot worse than that to get me angry with you."

The question of why bad things happen to people of integrity has plagued believers for millennia. Rabbi Kushner, in his book *When Bad Things Happen to Good People,* uses the book of Job to address this question. He says that the book of Job presents three truths: that Job is blameless, that God is good, and that God is omnipotent. Because of the calamity that has fallen upon Job, one of these truths must be wrong, and the purpose of the book of Job is to figure out which statement is false.

Christians suffering from depression often feel a sort of spiritual crisis as they seek to cope with their emotional pain. Did God inflict this illness on them as a punishment? Did God merely sit back and allow it to happen? Does God hold any interest at all in their suffering? If God does care, why doesn't God heal them?

Depression can separate us from God if we allow our anger to control us. Used creatively, it can also bring us closer to God. Depression forces people with busy lives to slow down, and sometimes that slowing down, that feeling of emptiness, can give God room to work. Depression, used creatively, can aid us in developing spiritual humility. We find that doing all the right things does not make us any more worthy of God's graciousness than people who do all the wrong things. Depression can help us to acknowledge that we have sinned, that our own righteousness has very little value, and that we must turn to God in order to become truly righteous.

Finally, depression can make us more sensitive to other people in pain. It can form a bond between ourselves and people we once avoided because we thought them "dysfunctional." When we come to the conclusion that our suffering does not have much to do with our inherent value as human beings, we can look beyond other people's dysfunctions and acknowledge their inherent worth.

We need to remember that God has not changed, even though our lives seem to have changed for the worse. While we may not be able to explain why God seems to allow us to suffer, we can rest somewhat in the knowledge that God loves us. Furthermore, God can take our anger and pettiness. It will not change the way God feels about us. After our tantrums, however, we need to consider whether we wish to reject God or draw nearer to God.

Things to Think About

Has living with depression affected your image of God? If so, in what way?

Have you ever felt anger towards God? Have you ever felt guilty afterwards?

Can you think of some ways that depression has changed you for the better? Can you think of some ways it has changed you for the worse?

Thinking of God as a loving parent, can you imagine how God responds to your suffering?

Prayer

God, help me to use my depression creatively instead of using it to push you away. Thank-you for loving me in spite of my anger. Amen.

12

Faithful in despair

Psalm 22:1-11

My God, my God, why have you forsaken me? Why are you so far from helping me, from the words of my groaning? O my God, I cry by day, but you do not answer; and by night, but find no rest. Yet you are holy, enthroned on the praises of Israel. In you our ancestors trusted; they trusted, and you delivered them. To you they cried, and were saved; in you they trusted, and were not put to shame. But I am a worm, and not human; scorned by others, and despised by the people. All who see me mock at me; they make mouths at me, they shake their heads; "Commit your cause to the LORD; let him deliver–let him rescue the one in whom he delights!" Yet it was you who took me from the womb; you kept me safe on my mother's breast. On you I was cast from my birth, and since my mother bore me you have been my God. Do not be far from me, for trouble is near and there is no one to help.

As Jesus hung on the cross, he did not say, "Even though I walk through the valley of the shadow of death, I will fear no evil, for thou art with me." He instead expressed his despair at God's abandonment of him with the words of the psalmist who had despaired centuries before him.

In fact, the writers of the Gospels used several verses from this psalm in association with Jesus' crucifixion. We can find verse 7 in Mark 15:29, verse 8 in Matthew 27:43, and verse 18 (not included in the above passage) in Matthew 27:35, Mark 15:24, Luke 23:34, and John 19:23-24.

One of the striking features of Psalm 22 is the vacillation between hope and despair. At first reading, this psalm seems almost schizoid. However, the alternation between expressions of despair and expressions of joyous praise is intentional. Notice that in the praise sections (verses 3-5, 9-10) the psalmist recalls God's past acts of graciousness. When the children of Israel cried out under the burden of their slavery in Egypt, God heard them and helped them escape. God sustained them as they wandered in the desert and brought them to the land of Canaan.

In verses 9-10, the psalmist remembers God's graciousness to him personally. God saw to it that the psalmist survived his birth and childhood and sustained him as he grew, his parents having entrusted him to God from the time he was born.

The psalmist recalls these past acts of graciousness because he can see no evidence of this grace in his current situation. As he lies suffering and near death (verses 14-18) his enemies gloat at his misfortune. If God intervened on the behalf of his ancestors and watched over him as he grew to adulthood, why doesn't God come now and save him from this wretchedness? He has trusted in God all his life as his parents taught him. So why does God not help him when he needs God most?

The psalmist's perceived desertion by God

has made him feel less than human, less than vertebrate even. His enemies taunt him. "God's favorite" has found himself in bad circumstances. If God really liked the psalmist so much, where is that God now? The psalmist despairs because he fears they might be right. Perhaps God really has deserted him.

His only defense and his only comfort is the memory of God's past saving acts to himself and his ancestors. He will continue to trust in God on the basis of these memories–and because he has no choice. No one else can help him.

Application

"Those who forget the past are doomed to repeat it" has become a familiar maxim, used most often in a political sense.

If we forget the circumstances which gave rise to Nazi Germany, we stand in danger, for example, of allowing another dictator to take power.

On a personal level, we need to remember the past not only to avoid making the same mistakes again but also so that we will remember the good things that have happened to us. If we forget God's graciousness to us in the past, when we look to the future we will not find ourselves able to trust in God's graciousness to us.

In Psalm 22 we find hope and despair on equally profound levels. We have learned to regard despair as an enemy of the spiritual life. Yet the psalmist's despair, as well as his hope, spring from the same deep faith in God. In our own spiritual journey, we do not need to regard our despair as an indication that we lack faith. Even deeply spiritual people like the person who wrote this psalm—and even our Lord Jesus Christ—felt despair.

What we need to learn is not to let our despair control us. When we feel gripped by hopelessness, we need to remember times we felt hopeless in the past. Better yet, we need to remember times in the past that our hopes were realized. If we set our despair against the backdrop of God's saving acts to ourselves as well as other people through the ages, we will see that God's graciousness is far greater than our sense of doom. Despair is a mortal emotion and will come to an end. God's graciousness lasts forever.

Things to Think About

Write down a list of issues that factor into your current feelings of depression (for example, loss of a loved one, stresses at work, anger towards a spouse). Now alternate between each of these issues a memory of God's past graciousness to you or your ancestors. Your own psalm might look something like one of the following:

> O God, I miss my father so much. There are so many things I long to speak to him about. There are so many times I need the support he used to give me. Why did you let him die of cancer?
>
> And yet I praise you for having given me a nurturing parent. You brought my grandparents over from Russia and blessed them with parenting skills, which my father, in turn, used to help me and my brothers.
>
> God, the office politics at work have become

> unbearable. Everybody is suspicious of everyone else. I have been betrayed by people I thought were my friends. We really need the money, so I can't quit. But the thought of going to work makes me cry every morning.
>
> And yet, I remember when I found that "perfect job" the year before I was married. I thought at the time you must have intervened in connecting me with that agency, because I loved every minute of the two years I worked there.
>
> God, I don't like being around my wife anymore. It seems that I cannot say anything without it exploding into an argument. We both want this marriage to work, but the harder we work at it, the more of a mess we seem to make.
>
> And yet, I remember our wedding and the sense of closeness we felt then. We were best friends. We thought our love for you would carry us through any hard times we faced.

Do you feel guilty when you feel despair? What are some ways that utter despair brings us closer to God? What are some of the ways it separates us from God?

Prayer

God, even in my despair I trust in you. I remember the good relationship we had in the past. Help my memories sustain me during the hard times. Amen.

13

Where is God?

Psalm 139:1-12

O LORD, you have searched me and known me. You know when I sit down and when I rise up; you discern my thoughts from far away. You search out my path and my lying down, and are acquainted with all my ways. Even before a word is on my tongue, O LORD, you know it completely. You hem me in, behind and before, and lay your hand upon me. Such knowledge is too wonderful for me; it is so high that I cannot attain it. Where can I go from your spirit? Or where can I flee from your presence? If I ascend to heaven, you are there; if I make my bed in Sheol, you are there. If I take the wings of the morning and settle at the farthest limits of the sea, even there your hand shall lead me, and your right hand shall hold me fast. If I say, "Surely the darkness shall cover me, and the light around me become night," even the darkness is not dark to you; the night is as bright as the day, for darkness is as light to you.

In contrast to Psalm 22, in Psalm 139 the psalmist does not need to remember God's past saving acts in order to sustain him as he despairs in the present. God's power and love are ever present. Indeed the psalmist could not escape from God even if he wished to, because God is everywhere.

Margaret Wise Brown wrote a children's book that seems to capture some of the relationship of the psalmist with God.

> Once there was a little bunny who wanted to run away. So he said to his mother, "I am running away."
>
> "If you run away," said his mother, "I will run after you. For you are my little bunny."
>
> "If you run after me," said the little bunny, "I will become a fish in a trout stream and I will swim away from you."
>
> "If you become a fish in a trout stream," said his mother, "I will become a fisherman and I will fish for you."
>
> "If you become a fisherman," said the little bunny, "I will become a rock on the mountain, high above you."
>
> "If you become a rock on the mountain high above me," said his mother, I will be a mountain climber and climb to where you are."

The story continues along in this vein until the young rabbit declares:

> "I will become a little boy and run into a house."
>
> "If you become a little boy and run into a house," said the mother bunny, "I will become your mother and catch you in my arms and hug you."
>
> "Shucks," said the bunny," I might just as well stay where I am and be your little bunny."
>
> And so he did."Have a carrot," said the mother bunny.

As a parent seeks tirelessly after a child, so God searches after us. The psalmist lists the extremes of his imagination. Sheol, the place in ancient Hebrew thought where the dead go, almost by definition is a place without the presence of God. While Sheol does not correspond exactly with our image of hell, finding God in Sheol would be as shocking as finding God in hell.

The wings of dawn may carry the psalmist from the farthest east to beyond the known world on the far horizon of the western sea. They cannot bear the psalmist away from God. Even if the psalmist finds himself in total darkness, a nothingness so profound as to eliminate all thoughts of creation, God will find him, for God alone can master the forces of dark and light.

Application

We do not expect to find God in depression. We may feel God in the sharp pain of grief or we may feel God supporting us in righteous fury. When we experience joy, we sense God's presence easily.

But depression, which may vacillate between dull resignation and senseless panic attacks, does not seem to leave much room for God. Can God really find us in our pit of self-absorption?

Is God there when we weep our tears? Surely we would not feel such loneliness and isolation if God were with us!

You can probably guess the psalmist's response. We only think we live in a darkness apart from God. God is with us there.

Things to Think About

As a child, did you experience the tenacious parenting skills of the mother bunny? Did you feel that your parents would never let you "run away?" Whether you did or didn't, how has your perception of your parents affected your perception of God?

List some states of mind or emotions in which you would not expect to find God. Imagine encountering God there. How would you respond?

Have you ever wanted to escape from God? Have you ever felt God totally absent in your life?

Prayer

God, give me the eyes to see you everywhere, even when my depression gets in the way of feeling your presence. Amen.

14

Hopes and dreams

Proverbs 13:12

Hope deferred makes the heart sick, but a desire fulfilled is a tree of life.

The Book of Proverbs belongs to a genre of Old Testament literature called wisdom literature. This type of writing also includes Job, Ecclesiastes, and a few of the Psalms. Most of the books of the Old and New Testaments are concerned with God's revelation to humankind. But wisdom literature seems to promote philosophical speculation. It asks why human nature is the way it is, and why people behave the way they do. Some of the wisdom literature in the Bible seems to bear more similarity to the wisdom literature of Israel's surrounding cultures (Babylonian, Persian, Greek) than to other books in the Bible.

Proverbs 13:12 belongs to a section called "The Proverbs of Solomon," which extends from Proverbs 10:1 to Proverbs 22:16. Following the form of most of the other bits of wisdom in this section, Proverbs 13:12 is antithetic, that is, it compares two inherent opposites.

Upon first reading, Proverbs 13:12 bears no relation to the surrounding verses. A natural reaction might be, "Yeah. So?" The intriguing part of the verse is that nothing modifies "hope" or "desire." The proverb does not distinguish between good hopes and desires or bad hopes and desires.

What if one hopes that a fascist government will come into power? What if one's deepest desire is for heroin?

We find references to the tree of life at both the beginning and end of the Bible. The tree of life grew in the Garden of Eden (Genesis 2:9, 3:22-24) and Revelation promises that it grows in paradise (Revelation 2:7, 22:2). One could conclude, probably, that only a good desire would merit a comparison to this tree, but in Hebrew the word can refer to both good and bad desires.

Assuming that the hope and desires are for positive things, how does a deferral of hope make the heart sick?

In his famous poem, "Harlem," Langston Hughes asked the question, "What happens to a dream deferred?" Using graphic imagery, he wondered whether such dreams dry up like raisins in the sun, fester like sores, stink like rotten meat, or just sag with unbearable heaviness. The poem concludes with the ominous question of whether a long-denied dream eventually explodes.

Hughes referred to a hope for dignity and equality denied to African Americans in the United States at the time he wrote. When people in power oppress others and deny them basic human rights, the hearts of both the oppressors and the oppressed become sick. As Langston Hughes hints at in his poem, deferring a hope for dignity has historically resulted in revolution and other types of violence.

On a personal level, we can think of many examples of hope deferred and what happens as a result. Think of the people who undergo surgery in the hope that they will cease to have seizures or to reduce crippling pain. What happens when the surgery helps just a little, but the people still have to face their disabilities for the rest of their lives? What happens to a couple when one wishes to marry and another isn't sure? What happens to a couple who long for a child and find out they will be unable to have one?

These may all be good hopes–hopes in accordance with God's will, and yet sometimes they go unrealized through no fault of the person who nourishes these hopes.

Is it better to have a hope deferred or a hope ended?

Application

Sickness of heart seems an apt description for depression, and many depressions can stem from a hope deferred.

So called "mid-life crises" often have to do with hopes left unfulfilled. Perhaps you thought by this time in your life you would have married and had a family, or published a book, or owned your own business, or gotten a degree. Perhaps you are angry that your life did not turn out the way you had planned. You may tell yourself it's silly to feel this way. You tell yourself you enjoyed the other things you did instead of doing what you had originally hoped for. But anger for hopes unfulfilled–and anger at our anger–sometimes turns inward and becomes depression.

Depression can subsequently cause a lack of hope or lack of desire. You do not expect to achieve what you hope for in any case, so why hope at all? It can be a painful task to unearth these hopes that lie dormant, not dead. And it can be even more painful to decide if you have a realistic chance of achieving them. But the process is necessary for healing.

If we decide that none of the hopes of our youth stand a chance of realization, remember we always have at least one hope left, "a sure and steadfast anchor of the soul" (Hebrews 6:19b). We will meet Christ again some day.

I have heard that the tree of life grows in his garden.

Things to Think About

Make a list of some of the hopes and dreams you had growing up. Were they all good hopes? Which were fulfilled? Would it be possible now for you to work on fulfilling some of the ones that weren't?

What would you consider negative hopes and desires?

Were some of the hopes left unfulfilled beyond your capacity to fulfill?

If you could have one of your fondest desires granted, what would it be?

Does thinking about a future reunion with Christ help or aggravate your depression? If the latter, what stands in the way of your anticipating the prospect?

Prayer

God, make all my hopes good hopes, and all my desires holy desires. Help me to see past my disappointments and focus on the hope of meeting Christ. Amen.

15

Pain doesn't last forever

Ecclesiastes 4:1-3

Again I saw all the oppressions that are practiced under the sun. Look, the tears of the oppressed–with no one to comfort them! On the side of their oppressors there was power–with no one to comfort them. And I thought the dead, who have already died, more fortunate than the living, who are still alive; but better than both is the one who has not yet been, and has not seen the evil deeds that are done under the sun.

John Bright, in assigning the Book of Ecclesiastes to the period after the Babylonian exile, refers to it as "questioning and gently skeptical" (*A History of Israel*, 3rd ed., Westminster Press, 1981, p. 438).

The passage cited above seems neither questioning nor gentle. It reeks of the dull certainty of despair.

This passage follows a section in which the writer has claimed that the only purpose for existence is that "all should eat and drink and take pleasure in all their toil" (Ecclesiastes 3:13). Anything else is "vanity." Human beings and animals alike return to the dust from which they were created after they die. There is nothing more.

The writer's denial of personal immortality accords with Jewish thought of the time (c. 300 B.C.E.). Human beings must enjoy any pleasures or rewards while they are still alive, because after death there is nothing.

Ecclesiastes 4:1-3 continues to spiral towards extreme pessimism. The writer mentioned the pleasure to be found in honest labor, but when he looked at the actual state of human affairs, he saw only wickedness and oppression.

From his detached viewpoint, the writer made an observation not otherwise mentioned in the Old Testament: Oppressors need comfort as well as the oppressed. In our post-psychological era we commonly wonder what deficiencies bullies experience in their home life. The phrase "it's lonely at the top" speaks to this insight of Scripture.

Verses 2 and 3 echo some of Job's laments. People commonly express gladness that Grandma didn't live to see the sad events of the world, congregation, etc. Ecclesiastes goes one step further and says the most fortunate beings are the ones who never existed.

Wisdom literature stands apart from most of the other literature in the Bible. Most of the Old and New Testaments explore–through narrative, history, poetry, and letters–God's interactions with humankind. Ecclesiastes is an extended reflection on the nature of existence.

Of what use is Ecclesiastes to the believer? We who believe that God rescued the Hebrew slaves from Egypt and sent Jesus Christ to redeem us–what edification can we possibly find in the pessimism of Ecclesiastes?

For one thing, most of what the writer of Ecclesiastes said is true. Much of human endeavor does spring from vanity and pride. The righteous do not always prosper on earth and the wicked often do. Abuse of power propagates misery throughout most of the world. And death comes to us all in the end.

Given the truth of these observations, one might remark that in order to be filled with the truth of God's grace, one must allow oneself to become empty first. Ecclesiastes lays bare the truth of human existence, creating a windswept plain as the writer blows away all pretenses of human ambition. When we are left with nothing, only then can we fully appreciate the reality of God's grace. The apostle Paul, in Philippians 3:8, catches some of this spirit when he says, "More than that, I regard everything as loss because of the surpassing value of knowing Christ Jesus my Lord. For his sake I have suffered the loss of all things, and I regard them as rubbish, in order that I may gain Christ."

To truly hear God, one must accustom oneself to quiet. To truly see God, one must accustom oneself to the dark. Before we can truly know God, we must forget the world and all the vanities therein.

Application

For those who have considered suicide, this text may strike some unwillingly responsive chords. Is the price of existence really worth the misery of facing our sad and sordid world?

While some may say that the selected text might aggravate one already suffering from suicidal tendencies, it needn't do so. Indeed, the suicidal person might even find a drop of comfort in it.

Most people who think they wish to die really wish to be out of pain. In fact, when they find themselves contemplating suicide, they feel appalled. Surely Christians would never contemplate ending their lives! They should be filled with the hope of Jesus Christ's return and the establishment of his kingdom. As Christians, how can we possibly consider killing ourselves when we know how much pain it would cause those who love us? The ensuing guilt for thinking of suicide subsequently feeds the depression, which in turn feeds the suicidal feelings.

One way to break out of this self-destructive cycle is to see in Ecclesiastes the confirmation that we are not alone. For thousands of years people have become overwhelmed by the futility of human existence.

Emily Dickinson once wrote:

> I measure every grief I meet
> With narrow, probing, eyes–
> I wonder if it weighs like mine–
> Or has an easier size.
> I wonder if they bore it long–
> Or did it just begin–
> I could not tell the date of mine.
> It feels so old a pain–
> I wonder if it hurts to live–
> And if they have to try–
> And whether–could they choose between–
> It would not be–to die....

Most people at some time in their life, however briefly, wished they were dead. Unfortunately, it is hard to find people who want to talk about it. The subject frightens many. We need to consider whether we want to confide too much in the people who are close to us. Saying that you want to die is a heavy burden to lay on a friend or family member. While they may express their love and support and try to think of things they can do to help you feel better, chances are they will feel helpless.

Suicidal feelings are a definitive symptom of depression. If you have them, there is no question that you need professional help. You may wonder sometimes if you ought to see a doctor for, say, a sore throat that has lasted for over a week, or persistent back pain, or an itchy scalp. Suicidal feelings are like severing a major blood vessel or breaking a bone or finding yourself suddenly blind. You need to see a doctor, therapist, or someone trained in pastoral counseling if you have these feelings.

Someone once told me when I was going through a particularly rough period of my life, "Suicide is a permanent solution to a temporary problem." You will not feel the pain you are feeling right now forever. Some day you will feel that the effort to keep on living was worth it. In the meantime, know that you are not alone and get help.

Things to Think About

Do you believe for yourself that it takes more courage to live or die?

What are some of the reasons you have not killed yourself?

If a friend told you he or she wanted to die, what would your reaction be?

What changes would be necessary in your life for you to wish to keep living?

Does knowing that many other people have felt suicidal at some time during their lives comfort you or does it make you feel even more depressed?

If you could share your feelings with anyone, with whom would you choose to share them? How do you think sharing these feelings would affect that person's life?

Prayer

God, I believe that you are neither afraid nor ashamed of my feelings. Give me the strength to do what I need to do. Guide me to people who can help. Amen.

16

When life isn't fair

Ecclesiastes 9:11-12

Again I saw that under the sun the race is not to the swift, nor the battle to the strong, nor bread to the wise, nor riches to the intelligent, nor favor to the skillful; but time and chance happen to them all. For no one can anticipate the time of disaster. Like fish taken in a cruel net, and like birds caught in a snare, so mortals are snared at a time of calamity, when it suddenly falls upon them.

Have a *nice* day.

Qoheleth, the name attributed to the author of Ecclesiastes, has an exceedingly grim worldview. Because much of what he says is true, we can forget that the swift usually do win their races, the strong win their battles, etc. The word translated as "chance" in verse 11 occurs one other time only in the Bible, in 1 Kings 5:4, where the NRSV translates it as "misfortune." We need to understand that when the strong and the wise do not win out, it is usually because something unexpected and unfortunate has happened.

In the 1972 Olympics at Munich, Jim Ryun, the world record holder for the 1,500-meter run, tripped in a qualifying heat. So he was unable to compete for a medal in the finals. When the Khmer Rouge took power in Cambodia in 1974, they systematically murdered the scholars and skilled workers in the country. As Qoheleth says, no one can anticipate a time of disaster. Sometimes life isn't fair. Sometimes bad things happen to good people.

In the conclusion of his book by that title, Harold S. Kushner writes:

> Is there an answer to the question of why bad things happen to good people? That depends on what we mean by "answer." If we mean "Is there an explanation which will make sense of it all?–Why is there cancer in the world? Why did my father get cancer? Why did the plane crash? Why did my child die?"–there is probably no satisfying answer. We can offer learned explanations, but in the end, when we have covered all the squares on the game board and are feeling very proud of our cleverness, the pain and the anguish and the sense of unfairness will still be there.
>
> But the word "answer" can mean "response" as well as "explanation" and in that sense, there may well be a satisfying answer to the tragedies in our lives. In the final analysis, the question of why bad things happen to good people translates itself into some very different questions, no longer asking why something happened, but asking how we will respond, what we intend to do now that it has happened (*When Bad Things Happen to Good People*, Schocken Books, 1981, p. 147).

What will we do to reduce the chances that genocide will happen around the world? What will we do to ensure that children do not wither away in the inner city? How will we support the members of our church body who suffer loss and illness?

Some calamities we can prevent. Some we cannot. When either occur, we need to learn to move from "Why did this happen?" to "How will I respond?"

Application

The origins of depression vary from individual to individual. The loss of someone or something important to us, or an alteration in our life's circumstances, often bring with them depression.

Responsible people try to address this depression by doing all the right things. Knowing that they are not feeling quite themselves, they may make extra efforts not to take their frustrations out on the people to whom they feel close. They may seek the help of a medical or psychological professional and scrupulously follow his or her suggestions. They may courageously face traumas of their past in counseling.

And still the depression does not budge. Given enough time, the person suffering from depression may begin to panic and wonder if he or she will feel miserable forever. The future becomes a horrifying place. Because we have seen the bad things that can happen to us that are beyond our control, we can anticipate terrible events occurring over and over again. Wars and famine, death and disease will come upon millions of people who have done nothing to deserve their fates. They will happen to people we love and probably to ourselves as well.

When we begin to anticipate disaster and fear the future, we need to take some time to detach and analyze our present circumstances. We may feel lonely now, but we can remember times when we have not felt lonely, and there is a good possibility we will have times in the future when we do not feel lonely. We or someone we love may get cancer in the future, but we do not have cancer now. We cannot assume we will have cancer in the future. Looking at the reality of our situation now, disencumbered by our emotional reactions, can help us to feel less fearful.

The writer of Ecclesiastes, while pessimistic, is not wrong. Calamities do fall upon mortals suddenly. To tell someone who is depressed to "look on the bright side" or to stop anticipating disaster is not really helpful. If we had such control over our emotions, we would choose not to feel depressed and frightened about the future.

Rabbi Kushner, however, offers an alternative way of thinking. Instead of fearing disasters in our future, we can ask ourselves, "How will I respond as a believer if these disasters occur?" In confronting our present reality we can ask ourselves, "How will I respond to this misery as a Christian?" instead of saying, "Why has this misery happened to me?"

Such alternative responses are the best answers we have available to us. We can look forward to the time when God will give us a more satisfying answer.

Things to Think About

Would you say you have an optimistic or pessimistic view of the future? Would you say that bad things happen to people more often than good things happen?

How much control do you think people have over their destinies?

How realistic do you think your assessment of yourself and your situation is? Do other people agree with your self-assessment?

Make a list of the ten worst things that could happen to you. How likely is it that each of these things might happen? How would you respond if these things did happen?

How do you respond to Kushner's quotation? How have you responded to the pain of your present circumstances? What are the good responses you have made? What are the bad or inadequate responses?

Prayer

God, help me to respond to my present reality in the way you would wish me to respond. Help me to face the future with the confidence that you will help me to respond to anything that might happen. Amen.

17

In spite of our faults

Isaiah 1:5-9

Why do you seek further beatings? Why do you continue to rebel? The whole head is sick, and the whole heart faint. From the sole of the foot even to the head, there is no soundness in it, but bruises and sores and bleeding wounds; they have not been drained, or bound up, or softened with oil. Your country lies desolate, your cities are burned with fire; in your very presence aliens devour your land; it is desolate, as overthrown by foreigners. And daughter Zion is left like a booth in a vineyard, like a shelter in a cucumber field, like a besieged city. If the LORD of hosts had not left us a few survivors, we would have been like Sodom, and become like Gomorrah.

In 722 B.C.E. the Assyrians captured Samaria, the capital of the northern kingdom of Israel, and the country called "Israel" ceased to exist. The other small nations in the area pledged allegiance to Assyria and became slave states. Other states, including Judah (the southern kingdom of Israel ruled by King Hezekiah), sought help from Egypt. Isaiah registered his disapproval for this foreign policy several times (see Isaiah 30:1-7).

Assyria cracked down on the Philistines,

Edomites, Moabites, and the other nations who had shifted support to Egypt. One by one, forty-six of the fortified cities supported by Egypt fell until only King Hezekiah was left, and he was trapped in Jerusalem. An account of the siege of Jerusalem may be found in Isaiah 36–37. Hezekiah ultimately surrendered, and Judah became a slave state.

In the eighth century B.C.E. there were no rules governing warfare like those we have today in the Geneva Convention. Even by ancient standards, the Assyrians treated the people in their conquered countries with unusual cruelty. Isaiah compared the nation of Judah to a servant nearly beaten to death for repeated offense. The rebellion mentioned in Isaiah 1 may refer to Hezekiah's conspiring with Egypt. It could also refer more generally to the continuing injustices Isaiah saw perpetrated against the poor and the worship of idols.

Whatever the nature of the rebellion, Isaiah makes clear the consequences of this rebellion. The nation is devastated; all the cities except Jerusalem have been destroyed. He compared Jerusalem to a lone female who is vulnerable to attack or rape because she has no family or clan to shelter her. Jerusalem, formerly a great city, has become like the rickety structures in vineyards and vegetable gardens used to protect the fruits and vegetables.

In verse 9, Isaiah ended his rebuke by comparing Judah's plight with that of Sodom and Gomorrah after God destroyed those cities. Interestingly, at this point Isaiah chose to identify with the people he rebuked. He shared in the disasters afflicting the Judeans.

Application

The logical lesson to be learned from this passage is that the desolation that nations experience in wartime comes as a result of moral failure. Extrapolating from a national level to a personal level, we can attribute our spiritual desolation to moral failures on our part.

To an important extent, this is true. If we use sex or money in ways that we know are immoral, the conflict with our conscience will undoubtedly produce depression. If we use people and violate relationships, we find ourselves isolated, lonely, and depressed.

However, the comparison is not that simple. The Nazis mowed down the smaller countries of Europe. What "moral failures" did these countries commit to justify the rape, torture, and havoc that the German armies perpetrated on them?

Again on a personal level, immoral decisions we make can affect our state of mind, but what about those people who earnestly endeavor to lead holy lives pleasing to God and still struggle with depression? What about those people who suffer personal tragedies to which the natural response is depression?

We cannot apply the words of Isaiah universally to modern national and personal situations. Yet the image presented in these verses remains compelling for those people experiencing spiritual and emotional desolation. When we feel depressed, we can easily feel that there is "no soundness" in us. Because our emotional state is unsound, we can easily experience physical unsoundness as well from stress-related conditions. Sometimes our perceptions of our physical reality can change as well. We can look in the mirror, and because we feel repulsive on the inside believe we look repulsive on the outside as well. We can become abnormally sensitive to people's reactions to us (for example, believing that they think us stupid because of something we said).

Thinking of ourselves as repulsive has the unpleasant power of self-fulfilling prophecy. When we view ourselves in this manner, we are not a lot of fun to be around, and some people might avoid us.

At these times it can be helpful to remember that God has seen us at our worst. God can see the ugliness lurking within us that no one else has seen. And yet, God loves us. We can engage in perverse sexual acts and abuse our children, and God still loves us. No matter how degraded and decadent we have become, God never finds a repentant heart repulsive.

It might be appropriate to look at our self-hate in light of God's love. In hating ourselves, do we fault God's judgment (if God only knew how horrible we really were...)? When we say God loves us while we hate ourselves, do the words become mere rhetoric? Are we better judges of our character than God is?

Things to Think About

Do you view your depression as stemming from a moral failure on your part? What are your behaviors that contribute to your depression? Does the knowledge that a change of behavior might alleviate or prevent your depression make you feel empowered or guilty?

Have you felt that you must have repulsed other people at some times in your life? What are some of the ways in which you felt your presence or behavior repulsed people? Have you ever found that people avoided you? Do you know for a fact that these people felt repulsed by you, or did you make an assumption as to how they felt?

If someone told you that he or she felt repulsive, what would your reaction be? How would you demonstrate to this person that you did not feel this way?

Prayer

God, sometimes I feel that there is no soundness in me anywhere. Give me the perception to feel your acceptance of me. Help me to act on the knowledge of your love for me. Amen.

18

Waiting for God

Isaiah 40:27-31

Why do you say, O Jacob, and speak, O Israel, "My way is hidden from the LORD, and my right is disregarded by my God"? Have you not known? Have you not heard? The LORD is the everlasting God, the Creator of the ends of the earth. He does not faint or grow weary; his understanding is unsearchable. He gives power to the faint, and strengthens the powerless. Even youths will faint and be weary, and the young will fall exhausted; but those who wait for the LORD shall renew their strength, they shall mount up with wings like eagles, they shall run and not be weary, they shall walk and not faint.

In 587 B.C.E. the Babylonians destroyed Jerusalem and carried off most of the powerful people and skilled workers to exile in Babylon. This was the second of three such deportations.

For nearly fifty years, the Jews remained in Babylon, grieving for their home. Psalm 137 records some of this grief as well as the anger at the Babylonians and the Edomites who had helped them plunder Jerusalem:

> By the rivers of Babylon—there we sat down and

> there we wept when we remembered Zion. On the willows there we hung up our harps. For there our captors asked us for songs, and our tormentors asked for mirth, saying,"Sing us one of the songs of Zion!" How could we sing the Lord's song in a foreign land? If I forget you, O Jerusalem, let my right hand wither! Let my tongue cling to the roof of my mouth, if I do not remember you, if I do not set Jerusalem above my highest joy. Remember, O LORD, against the Edomites the day of Jerusalem's fall, how they said, "Tear it down! Tear it down! Down to its foundations!" O daughter Babylon, you devastator! Happy shall they be who pay you back what you have done to us! Happy shall they be who take your little ones and dash them against the rock (Psalm 137:1-9)!

The exile in Babylon also gave the Jews, as they were now called, time to reflect on their relationship with God and what had gone wrong. Isaiah 40–55 was written for these exiles.

Part religious ritual and part custom, the Jewish people often recounted God's gracious acts to the Hebrews during the Exodus and conquest. Now some of their descendants in Babylon said that the days of God's intervention on behalf of Israel had come to an end. They had screwed up, becoming more interested in politics and wealth than in justice and faithfulness. As a result, God had allowed the destruction of Jerusalem. They had lived in Babylon for decades now, and God had sent no Moses to lead them home.

Isaiah 40 says that such thinking is foolish. The chapter emphasizes God's power as Creator. To doubt God's powerful intervention on behalf of the poor and weak was to doubt God's powers of creation.

The prophet told his people they must continue to wait, but not because God was going to take a while. Rather, God was acting for them all the time because they are a part of creation. God will give strength to all who believe.

The mystery of why God does not act immediately to correct injustices or support the people who love God continues from age to age. And yet all the tragedies in world history have not caused people to stop believing in God. In every age, there are those who can help us wait for God's revelation and give us the faith that God has not forgotten us.

Application

When we feel depressed for any length of time, it is easy to believe that God has forgotten us. When we pray and nothing happens, we can doubt that God really cares about us; we can even doubt God's existence.

During such times it can be helpful to consider creation. The plants and animals and people around us exist. The planet earth exists. We exist. The God of our ancestors had the power to create and sustain the universe.

The passage from Isaiah assures us that God does not forget creation. Maybe we may not understand why we have to wait so long for this power to bring about our healing, but heal us God will.

We can choose to let the waiting for God embitter us, or we can use the waiting time to empty ourselves of anger and despair, to allow the

Spirit to move within us, to listen for God's voice. When we feel our emotional strength returning—and it will return—when we wake up that first morning without a feeling of dread, we will know the wait was worth it.

Things to Think About

How long have you been depressed? Do you remember when it started? How long did your depression last the last time you had it?

How has your depression affected your relationship with God? What do you think God is like?

What doubts has your depression engendered? Do these doubts scare you? Why or why not?

Do you believe that God can heal you? Do you believe that God will heal you?

List some instances in both biblical and recent history of how God intervened on behalf of believers. Try to think of a mixture of both major acts of grace and acts of grace towards individuals. Has God ever intervened in your life?

Prayer

God, I believe you care for every part of your creation, including me. Bring me a relief for my weariness, and strength to walk in the direction you desire me to walk. Amen.

19

God hurts with us

Isaiah 43:1-7

***B**ut now thus says the LORD, he who created you, O Jacob, he who formed you, O Israel: Do not fear, for I have redeemed you; I have called you by name, you are mine. When you pass through the waters, I will be with you; and through the rivers, they shall not overwhelm you; when you walk through fire you shall not be burned, and the flame shall not consume you. For I am the LORD your God, the Holy One of Israel, your Savior. I give Egypt as your ransom, Ethiopia and Seba in exchange for you. Because you are precious in my sight, and honored, and I love you, I give people in return for you, nations in exchange for your life. Do not fear, for I am with you; I will bring your offspring from the east, and from the west I will gather you; I will say to the north, "Give them up," and to the south, "Do not withhold; bring my sons from far away and my daughters from the end of the earth– everyone who is called by my name, whom I created for my glory, whom I formed and made."*

The prophecies in Isaiah 40–55 assured the Jews in exile that they should not believe that God had forgotten them in Babylon. The God who had created the world and brought their ancestors out of Egypt would still act on their behalf if they were faithful.

Isaiah 43 expounds on this idea, but makes the relationship more intensely personal. Notice that the words of the prophet establish an "I-You" relationship between God and Israel. The use of the word translated as "redeemed" refers to the imagery of a person buying the freedom of a relative who has been sold into slavery.

The reference to God bringing the people through waters and rivers is a reminder of the Exodus experience. Just as God freed the Hebrew slaves and brought them safely through the waters of the sea, so will God free the people from their captivity in Babylon and bring them safely home.

The references to Egypt, Ethiopia, and Seba might imply the breadth of God's magnanimity. God is willing to go to the remote parts of the civilized world to collect the "ransom" for Israel. It could also indicate that at the time these verses were written, Cyrus the Persian had already embarked on his successful conquest of the territories adjacent to the Babylonian Empire. The Jews in Babylon, indeed many of the Babylonians themselves, looked forward to the Persians gaining control, because their policies towards the people they ruled were more lenient than those of the Babylonian kings. In any case, the nations of northern Africa mentioned in this passage were far wealthier and more cultured than the remnants of the kingdom of Israel. Yet, to God, the Jewish people had more value than the great wealth of all these nations combined.

Passages such as these form the basis for much of what has been called "liberation theology." Liberation theology's basic premise is that God has a bias for the poor and oppressed. God loves the weak and powerless most. Such statements are provocative, of course, and subject to dispute. In the context of Isaiah 43, however, one should note that the exile in Babylon did end, and God brought the Jewish people home.

Application

When we put our problems in perspective, our depression does not seem that important. Parents of young children die from disease or accidents. Nations go to war with one another. Dictators thrive on their injustices.

It is good to break out of our self-absorption long enough to see that the fate of the world does not hang on our misery. However, in doing so, we can make the mistake of believing that our problems are not important. Anything that keeps us from functioning as servants in God's kingdom is important.

Furthermore, we forget that the world's priorities are not God's priorities. The world would have seen the Hebrews in Egypt as a very minor race when comparing them to Egyptian pharaohs and all their achievements. The Egyptian, Assyrian, and Babylonian kingdoms wielded exponentially more power than the nation of Israel ever did. Yet who aside from a handful of archeologists now remembers the names of their mighty kings? And who remembers the names of Saul, David, and Solomon? According to archeological records of the Assyrians and the Moabites, the most powerful king of the northern Kingdom of Israel may have been Omri, yet he is dismissed by the Deuteronomic historian with these words:

> Omri did what was evil in the sight of the LORD; he did more evil than all who were before him. Now the rest of the acts of Omri that he did, and the power that he showed, are they not written in the Book of the Annals of the Kings of Israel (1 Kings 16:25-27)?

Again, who today remembers Omri–and who remembers David?

God loves us. As members of God's people, our feelings are important to God. God hurts when we hurt. Comparing our problems to those of a global scale, we may think that we rank low on God's list of priorities, but remember, the world's priorities are not God's priorities.

Things to Think About

Who are the "unimportant" people today in whom God takes a special interest? Can you think of another historical example of how an insignificant people or person changed the world?

Make a list of the ten most important concerns in your life. Try to avoid listing what you think ought to be your most important concerns. Choose things that affect you personally. Now make a list of what you think God's top ten concerns might be.

Are there any items common to both lists? How did you feel when you tried to imagine what God's priorities were? How does this affect your understanding of how God views your problems?

How do we reconcile our "specialness" in God's eyes with our desire to live and think humbly?

Who are the other "special people" in the world? Why are they special?

Prayer

God, I do not feel special or important. Give me the humility to understand that you love me anyway. Help me to choose my priorities as you choose them, instead of as the world chooses them. Amen.

20

Learning from depression

Lamentations 3:19-33

The thought of my affliction and my homelessness is wormwood and gall! My soul continually thinks of it and is bowed down within me. But this I call to mind, and therefore I have hope: The steadfast love of the LORD never ceases, his mercies never come to an end; they are new every morning; great is your faithfulness. "The LORD is my portion," says my soul, "therefore I will hope in him." The LORD is good to those who wait for him, to the soul that seeks him. It is good that one should wait quietly for the salvation of the LORD. It is good for one to bear the yoke in youth, to sit alone in silence when the Lord has imposed it, to put one's mouth to the dust (there may yet be hope), to give one's cheek to the smiter, and be filled with insults. For the Lord will not reject forever. Although he causes grief, he will have compassion according to the abundance of his steadfast love; for he does not willingly afflict or grieve anyone.

The Hebrew manuscript of Lamentations originally had no title. As with the first five books of the Hebrew Bible, it took its name from the first word, "How?" This word seems particularly suited in view of the nature of the book. How could God have allowed Jerusalem to fall when God had promised David that his kingdom would last forever (2 Samuel 7:16)? How could God have allowed the Babylonians to desecrate the temple? How could God have allowed the chosen people to starve in the streets of the ruined city?

The first two chapters of Lamentations mourn the situation of the people in Jerusalem who were left behind after the Babylonians destroyed it and carried "the best and the brightest" off to exile. The old, the sick, and the children starved in the streets and mourned for the loss of their loved ones. Lawless scavengers plundered what the Babylonians left behind.

The third chapter expresses the personal distress of an individual living in these desperate times. This person describes the situation in language reminiscent of the book of Job and some of the Psalms: "My soul is bereft of peace; I have forgotten what happiness is. So I say, 'Gone is my glory, and all that I had hoped for from the Lord'" (3:17-18).

In Lamentations 3:19, the lament begins to take on a different tone. Like wormwood and gall, his sufferings leave a bitter taste in his mouth.

However, he still has reason to hope. As do the words from Isaiah 40-55, the writer encourages the suffering remnants of Israel to wait for the Lord, whose love and faithfulness for these left-behind people is still renewed every morning. In verse 33, the word translated by the New Revised Standard Version as "anyone" can actually refer to humankind.

After describing his personal sorrows and personal hopes, the writer extends that hope to all people. The Lord does not wish to afflict people of any nation. The selected passage reflects a belief, both ancient and modern, that God causes afflictions to happen to people for their own good. If it took conquest and exile to teach the people of Judah that they needed to repent, so be it.

The belief that God causes bad things to happen to people raises a lot of sticky theological questions. How can a good God cause suffering? Even if many of the people of Judah did turn away from God, why did God punish the children and the faithful as well? No one, ancient or modern, has come up with a perfectly adequate response to these questions. However, even if we do not know why things happen, we know what God expects of us. We wait and we hope.

Application

To someone suffering from depression, the words from this passage could cause both hope and despair. In telling ourselves "the Lord will not reject forever," we imply that to some extent God has rejected us. Albeit unwillingly, we conclude that God has caused our affliction because we have been dreadfully bad.

Of course we have all sinned and fallen short of the glory of God (Romans 3:23). In fact, we may have done some dreadful things for which we must suffer consequences. In many cases, however, guilt contributes to the magnitude of the force field of anxiety and dread. There must be a reason why we feel anxious and fearful and sad most of the time. We must have done something to deserve our misery.

When I entered therapy again after a break of several years, my new counselor interrupted me as I described how I felt and said, "So Kathy, how are you going to use your depression?"

Her question confused me, and she explained that depression is the body's way of telling us that something is not working. If we do not take the time to slow down and examine the stresses in our life, depression will do the slowing down for us. Instead of viewing my depression as the enemy, I should view it as a teacher, this counselor suggested.

The writer of Lamentations may have had something of the same idea in mind when writing, "It is good that one should wait quietly for the salvation of the Lord, to sit in silence when the Lord has imposed it." Sometimes the best response to suffering is quietness and waiting. We can become so cluttered up by the details of ordinary life that we leave no room for the spirit of God to move in us, to comfort us, to guide us.

We do not need to view our depression as a punishment from God. Indeed, if believing this cripples our ability to approach God, we should not believe it. God forgives. If, after having asked forgiveness, we find that our depression continues, we need to try a fresh approach to the condition rather than continuing to beat ourselves up. "The Lord is good to those who wait for him, to the soul that seeks him." Depression may give us the time and space we need to seek God in earnest.

Things to Think About

How do you treat your depression? As an enemy? Friend? Illness? Emptiness? Space?

What have you learned from your depression? How have you changed as a result of your depression (become less judgmental? more bitter?)

What good things have happened in your life since the onset of your depression? Think hard. Do these things have any connection with your depression? Or did they happen in spite of it?

What are some ways you can use your depression for good?

Prayer

God, I believe you can work through all the bad things in life and make them come out for the better. Help me to use my depression in ways which will bring me closer to you. Amen.

21

Facing mental illness

Daniel 4:31-37

While the words were still in the king's mouth, a voice came from heaven: "O King Nebuchadnezzar, to you it is declared: The kingdom has departed from you! You shall be driven away from human society, and your dwelling shall be with the animals of the field. You shall be made to eat grass like oxen, and seven times shall pass over you, until you have learned that the Most High has sovereignty over the kingdom of mortals and gives it to whom he will." Immediately the sentence was fulfilled against Nebuchadnezzar. He was driven away from human society, ate grass like oxen, and his body was bathed with the dew of heaven, until his hair grew as long as eagles' feathers and his nails became like birds' claws. When that period was over, I, Nebuchadnezzar, lifted my eyes to heaven, and my reason returned to me. I blessed the Most High, and praised and honored the one who lives forever. For his sovereignty is an everlasting sovereignty, and his kingdom endures from generation to generation. All the inhabitants of the earth are accounted as nothing, and he does what he wills with the host of heaven and the inhabitants of the earth. There is no one who can stay his hand or say to him, "What are you doing?" At that time my reason returned to me; and my majesty and splendor were restored to me for the glory of my kingdom. My counselors and my lords sought me out, I was reestablished over my kingdom, and still more greatness was added to me. Now I, Nebuchadnezzar, praise and extol and honor the King of heaven, for all his works are truth, and his ways are justice; and he is able to bring low those who walk in pride.

King Nebuchadnezzar makes an unlikely, sympathetic hero. Remember, this is the man who ordered Shadrach, Meschach, and Abednego thrown into the fiery furnace for refusing to worship him. After listening to the king describe a dream (Daniel 4:1-27), Daniel warned him that his mighty ego would reap dire consequences and urged the king to repent. Instead, a year or so later, the king, while walking on the roof of his palace, said, "Is this not magnificent Babylon, which I have built as a royal capital by my mighty power and glorious majesty?" (4:30).

Daniel 4:31-37 tells us that even as these words were in the king's mouth, God sent the prophesied insanity upon the king. He was driven away and lived for a unspecified amount of time like an animal.

The Book of Daniel achieved written form in the second century B.C.E. and is included in the "Writings" section of the Hebrew Bible. At that time, the Greeks ruled Palestine in an oppressive manner. Worst of the rulers was Antiochus Epiphanes, who outlawed the practice of Judaism, torturing and executing those who defied him. The Book of Daniel would have inspired the Jews in Palestine by showing how their ancestors remained faithful to their God while exiled in Babylon, despite the capricious practices of a monarch with a monstrous ego.

Taking the selected text on its own, however, we have an interesting account of how the ancient world regarded insanity. People with mental illness were treated like animals. Think of the descriptions of the people whose mental illness Jesus healed, for example, in Mark 5:1-5:

> They came to the other side of the sea, to the country of the Gerasenes. And when he had stepped out of the boat, immediately a man out of the tombs with an unclean spirit met him. He lived among the tombs; and no one could restrain him any more, even with a chain; for he had often been restrained with shackles and chains, but the chains he wrenched apart, and the shackles he broke in pieces; and no one had the strength to subdue him. Night and day among the tombs and on the mountains he was always howling and bruising himself with stones.

Lest we congratulate ourselves on how far we've come since biblical times, we should consider our own century. In the 1920s and 1930s proponents of the eugenics movement in the United States advocated sterilization and incarceration for "mentally defective" people. The Nazis sent observers to the United States and used the American eugenics rhetoric to justify the extermination of the mentally retarded, mentally ill, and other people with disabilities. The first working models of the gas chambers later used in Auschwitz and Treblinka were developed in the mental institutions (*The Nazi Persecution of the*

Churches by J.S. Conway, Basic Books, 1968, pp. 269-272). Today in the United States many mentally ill people wander the streets, homeless and vulnerable to victimization.

Those who live according to the teachings of the Bible need to remember that we have an obligation to look after the weak and vulnerable in our society. Jesus not only healed those afflicted with mental illness, he interacted with them. He loved them.

Application

Insanity both fascinates and repels people. The first time we see a psychotherapist or the first time we start on antidepressant medications it may hit us: "Now I am mentally ill." We may remember the people we have seen roaming the city streets with dazed expressions and multiple shopping bags. We may think of how it frightened us to watch someone having a loud and angry argument with a person who wasn't there. We may remember the mysterious aunt or uncle who was sent away to an institution long before our time.

Those of us who manage to function in spite of our depression may look with fear upon those whose depression has rendered them unable to complete even simple functions. Worse, we may feel an odd sort of smugness. "At least I'm not that bad off," we might say.

One of the ways we can allow God to work through our illness is to use it to make us more sympathetic to others who suffer from mental disabilities. We who have successfully managed to live with and conquer our depression can give hope to those who have had less success. We who have felt repulsive and alienated from society can empathize with those whom society has in reality rejected.

Jesus loved people with disabilities and was not ashamed to associate with them. He did not consider them animals or regard them as "unclean." Jesus loves us as well and accepts us, no matter what degree of mental illness we possess. We can become vessels for that love. Our suffering can become the means by which we show Christ's love to others who suffer mental illness.

Things to Think About

From one to ten on a scale of mental illness, where do you place yourself? Where do you place mentally ill people you have known? Where do you place most of the rest of society?

Do you find that you feel more compassion for mentally ill people since you have started receiving treatment for depression? Do you feel more fearful? Are you afraid you might someday be as dysfunctional as a psychotic or schizophrenic person?

At what point does associating with people with mental disabilities become therapeutic for a depressed person, and at what point does doing so induce greater despair? What is the Christian approach to take when we feel too emotionally exhausted to help someone with disabilities more severe than our own?

Have you ever felt tempted to tell a depressed person to "snap out of it?" Has anyone ever said that to you?

I have a friend who once told me that we live in a crazy society. Just as the elderly and sick are more susceptible to environmental pollutants, so are some people more susceptible to "emotional pollutants" and they thus succumb to mental illness. Do you agree? If so, what are the "emotional pollutants" in our society?

Prayer

God, help me to accept others who suffer from mental illness just as you have accepted me. Amen.

22

Living in lonely times

Matthew 8:19-20

A scribe then approached and said, "Teacher, I will follow you wherever you go." And Jesus said to him, "Foxes have holes, and birds of the air have nests; but the Son of Man has nowhere to lay his head."

The phrase "Son of Man" has been the source of much debate among scholars. Jesus used the term to refer to himself many times. As a matter of fact, in the Gospels the phrase appears only in the words attributed to him. It seems to have several nuances of meaning, including "mortal one" (see Ezekiel 2:1) and that of a celestial or messianic figure (see Mark 13:26). Jesus consciously used the term when describing the sufferings he would have to endure. Those sufferings included homelessness.

We feel pity for the people we see wandering homeless in the streets of our city, and at times we feel overwhelmed when we consider the millions of refugees in the world today. However, there also exists in modern times a sort of romantic vision of the hobo or traveler who wanders from place to place with complete freedom, following the wind. The homelessness Jesus referred to had no such romantic overtones. It would have been considered scandalous, and marked Jesus as a member of the most lowly classes in society.

In biblical times, as now, the homeless were especially vulnerable to the wicked elements of society. For that reason, the Hebrew Bible emphasized that "strangers," "aliens," and "sojourners" merited special consideration for those who worshipped the God of justice. Consider the following scriptures:

> When you reap your harvest in your field and forget a sheaf in the field, you shall not go back to get it; it shall be left for the alien, the orphan, and the widow, so that the LORD your God may bless you in all your undertakings. When you beat your olive trees, do not strip what is left; it shall be for the alien, the orphan, and the widow. When you gather the grapes of your vineyard, do not glean what is left; it shall be for the alien, the orphan, and the widow (Deuteronomy 24:19-21).

> "Cursed be anyone who deprives the alien, the orphan, and the widow of justice." All the people shall say, "Amen!" (Deuteronomy 27:19).

> O LORD, you God of vengeance, you God of vengeance, shine forth! Rise up, O judge of the earth; give to the proud what they deserve! O LORD, how long shall the wicked, how long shall the wicked exult? They pour out their arrogant words; all the evildoers boast. They crush your people, O LORD, and afflict your heritage. They kill the widow and the stranger, they murder the orphan, and they say, "The LORD does not see; the God of Jacob does not perceive" (Psalm 94:1-7).

Like widows and orphans, strangers could be

abused because they did not live within the protection of a family or clan. Sometimes they had no legal rights. When the educated scribe approached Jesus and asked to follow him, Jesus told him to count the cost of discipleship. The scribe had to leave behind the security of his home if he truly wished to be one of Jesus' disciples. He had to leave behind the comfort that even dumb animals possess.

Jesus said that he and his followers had another, better home waiting for them in heaven. But the knowledge of this future home could not have completely comforted either Jesus or his disciples when they slept outside, huddling together for warmth.

Application

Modern people can experience a transience in jobs, homes, and friends that people in biblical times would not have considered quite "respectable." Transience can lead to a broader network of friends, or it can lead to acute loneliness. We live in very lonely times. People live by themselves and do not form the contacts with neighbors that used to be common. Relationships do not have the permanence they once did. Couples get divorced and families get left behind. People get promoted and leave friendships behind.

Even in a supportive church community, loneliness exists. Single adults often feel left out when their church activities seem geared towards families. However, loneliness is not restricted to singles. Loneliness can feel much worse within the context of marriage and family. Loneliness of the individual within a caring church community can produce feelings of guilt. Lonely people may feel they have no right to feel the way they do when they live in the midst of caring families and friends.

Depressed people can empathize with this guilt. Many of us have felt we have no right to be depressed, given our fortunate circumstances. By its very nature, depression produces feelings of isolation and loneliness. People see only our surface–the surface person who seems to "belong." Inside, we live thousands of miles from the place we belong. We may not even be sure that place exists anymore.

At such times it can be helpful to remember that this world is not our home. Jesus told us the location of our home in John 14:2, "In my Father's house there are many dwelling places. If it were not so, would I have told you that I go to prepare a place for you?" In a sense, all of the inhabitants of this earth are homeless until we reach God's house. Friends, family, and a loving church community can make this homelessness a little less lonely. And Jesus will remain with us until we die. He knows what it feels like to not belong.

Things to Think About

Make a list of the positive aspects of having a home (for example, feelings of safety). Now make a list of the negative aspects of having a home (for example, less freedom). Now list the positive and negative aspects of transience.

Do you feel that you are living "at home" or "in transience"? How do you feel about your situation? What are some ways God can work through your current situation?

Define "home." How do you imagine the worldly view of home differs from the heavenly view?

Have you ever felt you were living in exile or as a refugee? If so, how did that feeling change with the passage of time?

What are some ways you could reach out to the refugees and homeless in your current situation?

Prayer

God, you understand how it feels to not belong. Keep my eyes fixed on the true home I will have some day with you. Amen.

23

Lightening the load

Matthew 11:25-30

At that time Jesus said, "I thank you, Father, Lord of heaven and earth, because you have hidden these things from the wise and the intelligent and have revealed them to infants; yes, Father, for such was your gracious will. All things have been handed over to me by my Father; and no one knows the Son except the Father, and no one knows the Father except the Son and anyone to whom the Son chooses to reveal him. "Come to me, all you that are weary and are carrying heavy burdens, and I will give you rest. Take my yoke upon you, and learn from me; for I am gentle and humble in heart, and you will find rest for your souls. For my yoke is easy, and my burden is light."

This passage has a parallel in Luke 10:21-22, but only Matthew mentions Jesus' teachings as a yoke for his believers to carry. Most people associate yokes with the frames of wood or metal that connect two draft animals–usually oxen–together. In biblical times (and later), yokes could also refer to a frame fitted over the neck of one person by which that person could carry pails of water or other equally matched burdens. In New Testament times, the yoke symbolized submissiveness or servanthood.

In the Talmud, we find the yoke of the law or the yoke of the commandments referred to in a positive sense. In accepting the yoke of the law, believers put off the yoke of earthly rulers or life's hardships. The teaching in the selected passage has some of the same spirit. The yoke of Jesus is meant to better people's lives, not make them miserable.

The Jewish laws of the first century were never meant to be a hardship for the people who followed them. Indeed, the goal of the laws was to help people live holier lifestyles. As in all ages, however, the laws themselves became the focus of some people's religions rather than faithfulness to God, which these laws were meant to help people achieve.

Jesus, along with other first-century rabbis, notably Hillel, wanted people to get back into the spirit of the law. The simple people, the children who had not undergone the rigorous training of the scribes and Pharisees, sometimes had the advantage over the more educated Jews of their day. They did not have to "unlearn" the restrictions that others had so diligently cultivated.

Yet Jesus offered rest to all, the simple and the learned. Wise people carried heavy burdens as well as simple people. Jesus encouraged them to exchange the yokes that wearied them for one more manageable and more likely to help them get where they wanted to go.

Application

Life deals us various burdens–usually without a sense of fairness. We lose the people we love. We fail to achieve the goals we sought after. We suffer from various degrees of disease and pain. How we choose to carry these burdens determines how successful our lives will be.

We can choose the yoke of alcohol or drugs to help us carry our burdens. It may seem light the first few times we wear it. Then we discover that we are not carrying the burdens we thought we were carrying–we left them back at the place where our addiction started. And the yoke of our addiction has become heavier than any of the burdens we meant to carry with it.

Sometimes we make yokes out of the "shoulds" we have grown up with. "I should deal with my children this way, because this is the way good parents should deal with their children." "I should deal with my problems this way, because this is the way Christians should deal with their problems." Often we can make stacks of yokes from all the "shoulds" we have learned in our lives, and while they carry our burdens, they are as heavy to carry as the burdens themselves.

On the other hand, sometimes we can carry burdens that we would have thought humanly impossible to carry, because we have chosen the right yoke with which to bear them. Mother Teresa works in a "hopeless" situation among the dying in the slums of Calcutta, and yet she seems to bear the burdens of her work not only easily but with zest. Corrie Ten Boom and other Christians of the Nazi era faced torture and death in order to hide the people whom the Nazis had deemed unfit to live.

I had a friend who contracted breast cancer. Urged by the people of her church not to seek medical treatment, she prayed and sought help from faith healers. The tumor continued to grow. Ultimately, she had a mastectomy. She told me after the operation, "You know, I didn't see the miracle in the fact that the doctor discovered my tumor when it was the size of a pea. Maybe I wouldn't have needed to have my breast removed if I had allowed the doctor to act on that miracle. But," she continued cheerfully, "after the operation, all the nurses were amazed that I felt no depression. And that was a miracle, too."

What Jesus said about yokes in the first century holds true for people today as well. If our yokes are not easy, perhaps that is an indication that they are not of God.

Things to Think About

Is your depression the yoke by which you carry your burdens, or is it the burden itself?

What are the major burdens in your life right now? When does bearing them seem burdensome, and when does it seem like a privilege? What would happen if you put them down? What could you do to make the burdens lighter?

When Jesus refers to his burden, what do you think he means? Can you substitute that burden for one of the burdens you carry now?

Do you stack your yokes? How much help have they been in bearing your emotional burdens? Are some of the yokes more useful than others?

What are some of the "shoulds" in your life that have not been as helpful as you would have liked?

In what way could the yoke of Jesus make your burdens lighter?

Prayer

God, help me to sort through my yokes and find the one you have given me. Help me to discard all the burdens you do not mean for me to carry and all the yokes that you have not intended for me to use. Amen.

24

Help for the drowning

Matthew 14:22-33

Immediately he made the disciples get into the boat and go on ahead to the other side, while he dismissed the crowds. And after he had dismissed the crowds, he went up the mountain by himself to pray. When evening came, he was there alone, but by this time the boat, battered by the waves, was far from the land, for the wind was against them. And early in the morning he came walking toward them on the sea. But when the disciples saw him walking on the sea, they were terrified, saying, "It is a ghost!" And they cried out in fear. But immediately Jesus spoke to them and said, "Take heart, it is I; do not be afraid." Peter answered him, "Lord, if it is you, command me to come to you on the water." He said, "Come." So Peter got out of the boat, started walking on the water, and came toward Jesus. But when he noticed the strong wind, he became frightened, and beginning to sink, he cried out, "Lord, save me!" Jesus immediately reached out his hand and caught him, saying to him, "You of little faith, why did you doubt?" When they got into the boat, the wind ceased. And those in the boat worshiped him, saying, "Truly you are the Son of God."

The Gospel of Matthew probably achieved written form in the last third of the first century after Christ. The Christians in Rome were suffering from severe persecution at this time. No doubt this story offered comfort by reminding them that Jesus Christ could master even the weather. He would not forget them in their suffering.

Mark 6:45-52 and John 6:15-21 also associate Jesus' walking on the water with his miraculous feeding of the huge crowd that came to hear him preach. The man who could multiply loaves and fishes was not bound by the laws of nature as other people were. He was, in fact, the master of these laws.

Only in Matthew's account do we find mention of Peter also walking on the water. The story confirms that Peter had an impetuous nature. Jesus rebuked him more than once for acting or speaking rashly (see Matthew 26:33-35 and John 13:8, 18:10-11).

We can easily feel sympathy for Peter in this situation. How many of us have started walking across a narrow bridge or stood on top of a tall building and suddenly found ourselves paralyzed? We start out not realizing that we ought to be afraid and then our equilibrium (or lack of it) catches up with us.

Imagine yourself in the disciples' position. Out in a little boat in a storm, you and your friends are at the mercy of the wind and the waves. No longer able to steer the boat and head toward land, you strive just to stay afloat.

You have spent a sleepless night trying to keep the boat from capsizing. In the early hours of the morning you look out and see someone or something coming toward you. You blink and shake your head a few times, thinking that this thing is just a product of your exhaustion. You look again and see that the thing is Jesus. "Oh good," you say, "it's only Je– Wait a minute! People don't walk on the water. Live ones, anyway. So that must mean– Uh-oh."

Peter, of course, liked to take risks. How do you suppose the water felt when he stepped out of the boat? Was it cold? Did it sting? Did he bob up and down like a corked bottle on the crest of each wave, or did the waves splash over his head as he stood there? Why hadn't he noticed the strong wind before he stepped out of the boat? How many steps did he take before he told himself, "This is too dangerous. I can't do this. Lord save me!"

Jesus' words seem harsh. "You of little faith, why did you doubt?" Notice, however, what he does before he speaks those words. He reaches out his hand and immediately grabs Peter to keep him from drowning.

He does not stand there and say, "Oh come on, Peter. I know you can do better than that." Or "I'm not going to help you because you need to learn to help yourself. You'll thank me some day for not pulling you out right now." Or "Would you just quit whining? It was your idea to come out and walk on the water. I didn't ask you to do it."

Jesus does not rebuke Peter until he is safely out of the water.

Application

Like Peter, it is easy for us to think that we are ahead of where we actually are spiritually. We have prayed diligently and earnestly sought the Lord's will for our lives. We have taken certain risks–emotional, financial, and otherwise–to help build God's kingdom.

When depression strikes, suddenly our spiritual coping devices don't seem to work any more. We praise God. We pray. We look to the Bible for answers. But we still find ourselves out in the water, battered by waves and sinking fast.

We need to acknowledge that we are not as spiritually evolved as we thought. We can't walk on water. We cannot fight our emotional battles by ourselves. Our faith is not strong enough to save us.

But God is. God will not let us drown in our depression. It may be a long time before we see land again or even before we make it back to the boat, but God will hold on until we get there.

Things to Think About

What used to help you when you felt depressed? Praying? Singing? Talking with friends? Why don't they seem to work any more?

Which portion of today's story best symbolizes where you are right now? Are you fighting the waves in your boat? Are you out in the water but sinking fast? Are you out in the water and desperately clinging to God's hand?

If you do not believe that God will keep you from sinking, is there someone you know who will believe it for you until you are strong enough to believe it for yourself?

Prayer

God, I believe you will save me from drowning in my despair, just as you saved Peter from drowning in the sea. Amen.

25

Learning to love myself

Mark 5:25-34

Now there was a woman who had been suffering from hemorrhages for twelve years. She had endured much under many physicians, and had spent all that she had; and she was no better, but rather grew worse. She had heard about Jesus, and came up behind him in the crowd and touched his cloak, for she said, "If I but touch his clothes, I will be made well." Immediately her hemorrhage stopped; and she felt in her body that she was healed of her disease. Immediately aware that power had gone forth from him, Jesus turned about in the crowd and said, "Who touched my clothes?" And his disciples said to him, "You see the crowd pressing in on you; how can you say, 'Who touched me?'" He looked all around to see who had done it. But the woman, knowing what had happened to her, came in fear and trembling, fell down before him, and told him the whole truth. He said to her, "Daughter, your faith has made you well; go in peace, and be healed of your disease."

The scene in which the woman receives the healing power from Jesus occurs in the middle of another story. Jesus has gone to heal the daughter of Jairus, a leader of the synagogue. No doubt Jairus, Jesus, and his followers felt some urgency to get there. Jairus had told them his daughter was dying. The people thronging about them may have slowed them down. In any case, among these jostling crowds of people, one person touched the fringes on his garment, and Jesus immediately knew.

Why would the woman have done this secretly instead of simply asking Jesus to heal her? Consider this passage from Leviticus:

> If a woman has a discharge of blood for many days, not at the time of her impurity, or if she has a discharge beyond the time of her impurity, all the days of the discharge she shall continue in uncleanness; as in the days of her impurity, she shall be unclean. Every bed on which she lies during all the days of her discharge shall be treated as the bed of her impurity; and everything on which she sits shall be unclean, as in the uncleanness of her impurity. Whoever touches these things shall be unclean, and shall wash his clothes, and bathe in water, and be unclean until the evening (Leviticus 15:25-27).

Jewish women were ceremonially unclean one to two weeks out of every month. During their menses, women pretty much gained the status of lepers. The woman in this story had spent twelve years of her life as an unclean outcast. How long had she lived without any human touch other than that of the doctors from whom she sought help? (And perhaps the doctors didn't touch her. Maybe they just told her what to do, handed her some herbal remedy, and took her money.)

Jesus' reaction was unexpected. Given the circumstances, he could have recoiled in horror. This woman had made him ceremonially unclean. He could have ripped off the outer garment she had touched and cast it away. He could have sought the closest place where he could go to bathe and attempted to cleanse himself from the impurities she had placed on him.

Instead he told the woman, who was trembling in fear at her audacity, that her faith had made her well. He called her "daughter," not "woman." Her trust in him had created a special relationship between them. He cared what happened to her. Imagine how these words must have sounded to a woman who had lived as an outcast for twelve years. Jesus followed up the healing of her physical condition with kind words of healing for the years of emotional abuse she had suffered.

The story continues with people from Jairus's house coming to tell him that his daughter had died. The woman had demonstrated to the crowds the power of faith. Her healing gave added emphasis to Jesus' words, "Do not fear, only believe" (Mark 5:36). Jesus then proceeded to bring the little girl back from the dead.

Application

Not surprisingly, people suffering from depression usually struggle with low self-esteem. At certain points when despair overwhelms us, we can become quite riddled with self-loathing.

People who know us may have no idea that we hate ourselves so much. Indeed, they may feel genuinely astonished if they find out, and they may proceed to list all our fine qualities. Instead of boosting our self-esteem, these words may convince us that if people really knew us, they wouldn't like us anymore.

On the other hand, self-loathing can become a self-fulfilling prophecy. No one enjoys listening to people spew out all the things they most detest about themselves. Given enough time, people will start avoiding us, which in turn, convinces us of how loathsome we really are.

At times such as these, we need to recall that God commanded us to love other people as we love ourselves. If we cannot love ourselves, we cannot follow through on this commandment. Furthermore, God loves us. To continue hating ourselves is to question God's judgment. Dare we say that God is mistaken? that if God really got to know us, God would hate us as much as we do ourselves?

People feeling self-loathing can't just "snap out of it" and start loving themselves. Self-hate builds up after years and years of emotional wounds that never fully heal. It does not go away easily. However, when we begin to have these negative feelings, we can make a conscious effort to think of Jesus and the love he showed us in his death. We can remember that he did not feel revulsion for the people his society considered unclean. He touched lepers. He reached out to the mentally ill without fear. He called the woman with the hemorrhage "Daughter." Perhaps his acceptance of outcasts healed them as much as his miraculous cures of their physical conditions did.

When we cannot view ourselves as anything other than repulsive, we must remember that

Christ does not view us that way. We need to have the humility to admit that his judgment is better than ours.

Things to Think About

Who are the outcasts of our society (people with AIDS, homosexuals, homeless, etc.)? Who are the people who make you most uncomfortable? Whom do you try to avoid?

Can you think of some times when you felt "unclean"? What helped you to feel restored?

Can you think of some times when your low self-esteem drove people away?

Make a list of the things you like least about yourself. Now make a list of the things you like most about yourself. How did you feel when you wrote out these lists? Which list was harder? Why?

Have you ever loved someone with severe mental, emotional, or physical disabilities? Was it hard for you to love him or her?

Prayer

God, you have loved and accepted me unconditionally. I cannot match your divine love, but give me the strength to accept, with love, myself and others. Amen.

26

I believe; help my unbelief

Mark 9:17-27

Someone from the crowd answered him, "Teacher, I brought you my son; he has a spirit that makes him unable to speak; and whenever it seizes him, it dashes him down; and he foams and grinds his teeth and becomes rigid; and I asked your disciples to cast it out, but they could not do so." He answered them, "You faithless generation, how much longer must I be among you? How much longer must I put up with you? Bring him to me." And they brought the boy to him. When the spirit saw him, immediately it convulsed the boy, and he fell on the ground and rolled about, foaming at the mouth. Jesus asked the father, "How long has this been happening to him?" And he said, "From childhood. It has often cast him into the fire and into the water, to destroy him; but if you are able to do anything, have pity on us and help us." Jesus said to him, "If you are able!–All things can be done for the one who believes." Immediately the father of the child cried out, "I believe; help my unbelief!" When Jesus saw that a crowd came running together, he rebuked the unclean spirit, saying to it, "You spirit that keeps this boy from speaking and hearing, I command you, come out of him, and never enter him again!" After crying out and convulsing him terribly, it came out, and the boy was like a corpse, so that most of them said, "He is dead." But Jesus took him by the hand and lifted him up, and he was able to stand.

This story immediately follows the account of Jesus' transfiguration, in which Jesus took Peter, James, and John up a mountain. There, his robes became dazzlingly white and he conversed with Moses and Elijah.

Some have seen a parallel in this story with that of Moses coming down the mountain after receiving the Law. Just as Moses found confusion and idolatry when he came down, so did Jesus find his remaining nine disciples arguing with a crowd of people when he came down the mountain. Apparently, these disciples had been unable to exorcise the demon that had afflicted the boy with seizures. Perhaps their failure drew unwanted criticism from the crowd. Perhaps some of the crowd were telling the disciples what to do next, which only annoyed the disciples more.

Jesus, fresh from the mystical experience on the mountain, assumed a businesslike approach in his response to human need. We do not know whom Jesus called a "faithless generation." Perhaps it included all the people present.

Nevertheless, his rebuke did not prevent the father from seeking his help. If you have ever known someone with an uncontrolled seizure disorder, you know how frightening these seizures can be for the person suffering them and his or her family. To know that you could be crossing a busy street and have a seizure in the middle of traffic, or holding a pan of boiling liquid, or working with sharp tools–the agony of the boy's father is very real. He had not disowned his son or driven him into the wilderness as some families did to people with unexplained "demonic" fits. He loved his child. If it were only possible for Jesus to heal him.

And then Jesus asked something of the father in return, and it was more than he could give. Perhaps he had taken his son to other healers and encountered nothing but failure. Perhaps he had prayed earnestly to God since the seizures first started years ago and nothing happened. Now Jesus asked him to believe that he could heal his son. The father knew that he was not up to it, but he gave what he could. He wanted to believe and asked Jesus to pick up the slack of what he couldn't believe.

And Jesus healed the boy.

"I believe; help my unbelief," has a liturgical ring to it. Many people think of the words as a sort of abstract theological expression and think that the "belief" pertains to the existence of God.

In the context of this passage, the "belief" mentioned is much more concrete. Jesus told the father that he must believe that Jesus could heal his son. The father, knowing that his son's healing somehow hung on his faith, wanted to believe that Jesus could indeed heal his son, but he doubted his own ability to believe sufficiently that such a miracle could occur.

Application

People suffering from depression may assume a defensive posture when asked if they have prayed to God to heal them. Christians, in particular, may have been told by people trying to help that if they would just get right with God, they would be healed from their depression. When they have prayed daily for healing, suggestions like these can make Christians feel guilty about their inadequate relationship with God, and the guilt can subsequently make them feel more depressed.

Before you dismiss hope in divine intervention as futile, however, you should ask yourself, "Have I really prayed for healing? Do I really believe God can heal me? Have I asked friends and family to pray for me?" It is one thing to seek God's intervention and face possible disappointment when God does not heal us miraculously. It is another thing not even to seek healing from God because we do not think it will help.

We do not always feel loving towards the people closest to us, and yet, we can choose to treat them lovingly. Putting our love into action often results in our recovering the loving attitudes we thought we may have lost.

Faith works the same way. Even when we feel riddled with doubt, we can still act as though we have faith, and in doing so, the faith we did not think we had becomes a part of our conscious self. Interestingly, whether the faith brings about the miraculous cure does not always affect whether our faith becomes strengthened by prayer. My friend with breast cancer did not experience miraculous healing. Her tumor continued to grow, despite the prayers of her church and the intervention of a faith healer. Yet after her mastectomy, her spiritual strength was greater than it had been before the operation. Somehow, in those many months of wrestling with doubt and fear, she had encountered God. If she had had it to do over again, she would have had the operation sooner. She would have chosen not to lose her breast. But God worked through that tragedy and made her a stronger person, more open to the Spirit.

We never pray in vain. Any sincere attempts to communicate with God and listen to God's leading have validity, no matter how clumsy or stumbling. Sometimes healing does come instantly to those who pray. Sometimes it comes much later, but all healing is miraculous, whether it comes as a result of prayer, psychotherapy, medicine, or a combination of the three.

We have chosen to follow Christ, and that means we continue following even when our faith wanes. We have chosen to believe that God cares about us. That means acting as if we believe it. God will take care of our unbelief.

Things to Think About

Name some specific examples of how God heals. Do some forms of healing have more validity than others?

Think of the people who love you and who would intercede on your behalf with God. Picture them in the crowd when Jesus comes down from the mountain and his disciples have failed to heal you. What would the people who love you say to Jesus on your behalf?

Say, "Lord I believe; help my unbelief," with different emotional inflections (sadness, anger, weariness, hopefulness, etc.). How does the meaning change with each different attitude?

Do you blame yourself when you don't get the

results you prayed for? What would you tell someone else who told you he or she had not been healed as a result of a lapse in faith?

Prayer

God, I believe that you will heal me. Help my unbelief. Amen.

27

Strength to make changes

Mark 10:17-22

As he was setting out on a journey, a man ran up and knelt before him, and asked him, "Good Teacher, what must I do to inherit eternal life?" Jesus said to him, "Why do you call me good? No one is good but God alone. You know the commandments: 'You shall not murder; You shall not commit adultery; You shall not steal; You shall not bear false witness; You shall not defraud; Honor your father and mother.'" He said to him, "Teacher, I have kept all these since my youth." Jesus, looking at him, loved him and said, "You lack one thing; go, sell what you own, and give the money to the poor, and you will have treasure in heaven; then come, follow me." When he heard this, he was shocked and went away grieving, for he had many possessions.

The man in this story made haste to catch up with Jesus before he set out on a journey. Referred to as a "young man" in Matthew and as a "ruler" in Luke, he may have wished to join Jesus' disciples and follow him.

Jesus gave him a rude awakening. First he criticized the young man for addressing him respectfully. Saying that the man should not call him "good" raises some difficulties for the modern reader, but Jesus' statement, "No one is good but God alone," would have expressed a characteristic attitude of any devout Jew of the first century.

Secondly, Jesus listed the six commandments that deal with how God wants human beings to interact with each other. No doubt the man wanted something a little more advanced. He knew the Ten Commandments. Moreover, he had conscientiously kept all of them since he was a young man. He did not boast of goodness. He really had followed these commandments carefully since the time of his Bar Mitzvah.

When Jesus looked at the man, he saw his sincerity and loved him, no doubt seeing the same possibilities in him that he saw in certain fishermen and tax collectors. So Jesus named the one last requirement, and the man, to his own personal grief, could not bring himself to meet it. As a faithful Jew, he would have consistently given generously to the poor anyway, but Jesus' requirements were too stringent. They were, in fact, shocking. Notice, however, that the man did not argue with Jesus. He acknowledged his failure and walked away. Jesus then used the opportunity to teach his disciples about the dangers inherent in wealth.

If Jesus had told the man to perform some complex ritual, to set up a system for fasting and prayer, he might have jumped at the chance. As it was, Jesus' answer was simple, but extremely difficult.

Application

Simple solutions to problems are rarely easy to carry out. The simple solution for an alcoholic's problem is for the alcoholic to stop drinking. Some other "simple" solutions may include: "Go into therapy." "Lose weight." "Forgive your parents." "Start on a medication regime." "End your relationship with _____."

Consider the following quotation from Doris Janzen Longacre's *Living More With Less* (Herald Press, 1980, p. 17): "The trouble with simple living is that, though it can be joyful, rich and creative, it isn't simple. Less of what? More of what? And for whom? Every day the average tradesperson or homekeeper makes a hundred small decisions which, if you stop to think about what causes what, becomes maddeningly complex."

Likewise, arriving at the simple solution to our depression can be maddeningly complex. The simple solution to our depression is to "snap out of it." And strangely enough, sometimes it is that simple. Sometimes people really do just snap out of their depressions, usually after having had a strong emotional experience, such as visiting a foreign country or seeing someone coping with much greater problems.

More often, though, they find themselves unraveling a complex web of family history, stress, emotional disturbances, and physical ailments. Sometimes when a person suffers from a lot of free-floating dread and anxiety, discovering the problem is complex enough; discovering the solution seems impossible. Usually counseling and medication do not help immediately, and the process of healing becomes very involved and gradual.

Remember that Jesus loved the man who could not give up his wealth. He knows that giving up aspects of our lives is hard. He knows that change is scary. When we know what holds us back from healing, he will give us the strength to get rid of it.

Things to Think About

What are some "simple things" you could change in your life that would aid in your healing? What do you find hardest about changing them? If you had the ability to change all these things tomorrow, how would your life change?

Make a list of things you could change in your life that would help you respond to your depression. Pick one thing on the list that you will change tomorrow.

Why is it easier to do things that prolong our depression than it is to do things that prevent or help it?

Prayer

God, I want to change. Give me the strength to give up the things that keep me from changing. Amen.

28

God knows what it's like

Mark 14:32-42

They went to a place called Gethsemane; and he said to his disciples, "Sit here while I pray." He took with him Peter and James and John, and began to be distressed and agitated. And said to them, "I am deeply grieved, even to death; remain here, and keep awake." And going a little farther, he threw himself on the ground and prayed that, if it were possible, the hour might pass from him. He said, "Abba, Father, for you all things are possible; remove this cup from me; yet, not what I want, but what you want." He came and found them sleeping; and he said to Peter, "Simon, are you asleep? Could you not keep awake one hour? Keep awake and pray that you may not come into the time of trial; the spirit indeed is willing, but the flesh is weak." And again he went away and prayed, saying the same words. And once more he came and found them sleeping, for their eyes were very heavy; and they did not know what to say to him. He came a third time and said to them, "Are you still sleeping and taking your rest? Enough! The hour has come; the Son of Man is betrayed into the hands of sinners. Get up, let us be going. See, my betrayer is at hand."

In the stained-glass windows depicting Jesus in the Garden of Gethsemane, we see a somber and heroic figure kneeling in prayer, his face illuminated by a rich light. The reality of the scene described by Mark is far less picturesque.

The English words "distressed and agitated" do not adequately convey the emotions expressed by the Greek. "Appalled and horrified" might come closer. If you compare the different English versions of the verse, you will find the words translated in several different ways. Jesus knew that the end had come. He knew that he would soon experience death by slow torture, and the full realization of the pain he would feel had overwhelmed him. He wanted to die right away, so he would not have to face the brutality of the Roman guards. He did not sedately kneel to petition his Father; he threw himself on the ground and begged for God to not make him have to go through with his crucifixion.

He knew that his disciples could not save him from what would come, but if they would just stay with him, share this time of intense fear and sorrow—just be there—maybe this lonely night would be a little more bearable. But it had been a stressful week for them: the triumphal entry into Jerusalem, Jesus' strange teachings about the end times and about his own death, his gloomy predictions that they would fail him. Although they had protested their loyalty to Jesus, and may have imagined themselves leaping to his defense if anyone tried to hurt him, they did not grant him a simple request: that they remain awake with him in his loneliest hour.

The scene at Gethsemane shows Jesus at his most human. We cannot properly understand the miracle of Easter, if we do not share in Jesus' utter horror and loneliness on the night he was betrayed.

Application

I once was involved in a relationship with someone I loved deeply. That person subsequently rejected me. As I cried out to Jesus in my anguish, I remember saying, with fury, "What do you know about rejection?"

The answer came back swiftly. Not only did Jesus completely understand rejection, he understood rejection by the people he loved most. He understood the paralyzing fear of a grim future. He understood what it felt like to ask God to save him from his pain and then to hear no response. He understood feeling abandoned by his best friends. He understood that he would have to suffer alone–and perhaps there can be no lonelier feeling than that.

It may seem melodramatic to compare our anxiety and depression to Jesus' experience in Gethsemane. Certainly the degree of our suffering does not compare. But that fact in itself can help us feel less alone. Jesus knows what it feels like to suffer from panic and loneliness. He knows it far better than we do. His understanding of our suffering far exceeds our own ability to understand our suffering.

Jesus did not question why he and the rest of humanity had to face suffering. He accepted them as a part of human existence. Being human, he shared in these sufferings.

We need to remember that Gethsemane was not the end of the story. Neither are our sufferings the end of our story.

Things to Think About

Have you ever felt that God does not listen to your prayers? What is your response to people who tell you you should pray for healing?

What times in your life have you felt the most scared or the most lonely?

Have you ever felt like your friends let you down? Have you ever felt abandoned by the people you loved? How did you respond?

Does it help you to think that Jesus has suffered in the same way you have? Why or why not? Do you have a sense that Jesus participates in your sufferings now?

If you were able to address Jesus face to face and talk to him about your depression, what do you think he would say to you?

Does thinking about Jesus' experience in Gethsemane make you feel that he understands you, or does it make you feel guilty for making the comparison?

Prayer

Jesus, I believe you understand how I feel. Help me to think of my depression as temporary. Help me show the understanding to others that you have shown to me. Amen.

29

Turning fears over

Luke 12:22-31

He said to his disciples, "Therefore I tell you, do not worry about your life, what you will eat, or about your body, what you will wear. For life is more than food, and the body more than clothing. Consider the ravens: they neither sow nor reap, they have neither storehouse nor barn, and yet God feeds them. Of how much more value are you than the birds! And can any of you by worrying add a single hour to your span of life? If then you are not able to do so small a thing as that, why do you worry about the rest? Consider the lilies, how they grow: they neither toil nor spin; yet I tell you, even Solomon in all his glory was not clothed like one of these. But if God so clothes the grass of the field, which is alive today and tomorrow is thrown into the oven, how much more will he clothe you–you of little faith! And do not keep striving for what you are to eat and what you are to drink, and do not keep worrying. For it is the nations of the world that strive after all these things, and your Father knows that you need them. Instead, strive for his kingdom, and these things will be given to you as well."

This passage is part of a section on the responsibilities and privileges of discipleship. The text applies easily to anyone who truly wishes to live the Christian lifestyle. It follows the parable of the rich fool who pulled down his barns to build larger ones so that he might "eat, drink, and be merry."

Jesus wanted his followers to take a different approach. Their attention should focus on God's kingdom, and their needs would be provided for. Verse 30 notes that the pagan Gentiles worried about things like food and clothing because they did not know God. Good Jews know that God is a father who will provide for his children.

Jesus did not say that his followers should not work to provide food and clothing for themselves and their followers. He was not an ascetic. It is the anxiety over meeting their needs that he preached against.

Neither did Jesus say that God would provide believers with gourmet feasts and designer clothing. God would see to it that their basic needs were met. Again, followers do not have to split hairs over whether these things are wants or needs. They should trust God completely to know what they need and to provide for these needs. They have more important things, like kingdom-building, to concentrate on.

Application

For someone who experiences anxiety attacks, the selected passage can arouse feelings of guilt and frustration. Why doesn't Jesus just tell us not to be bald or short or to have blue eyes? Those of us living within that force field of low-grade anxiety may feel that we have inherently failed God because we have continued in our anxiety despite the warning against it. We may feel that the anxiety is so much a part of us that we could no more stop worrying than we could stop breathing.

As a teenager I remember thinking about what it would be like to live without a constant sense of dread. I concluded that if I were not depressed I would not be myself, because my depressions seemed an integral part of my personality. During my freshman year in college, after walking around in a daze of happiness for a few weeks, I realized that my identity was not tied up with my depression. In fact, I realized that I had become more truly myself. The depression and anxiety had suppressed me, not described me.

We may feel that we have no control over our anxiety, but this is a false belief. Often simply forcing ourselves to sit down and face our fears, even pinpoint what they are, can help us to conquer them. We need to ask ourselves whether our anxiety relates to something that has happened or something that might happen. If what we fear has not happened yet, we need to acknowledge to ourselves that what we fear does not exist. Whether it might someday exist is irrelevant for the purpose at hand. Separating reality from our perception of reality can go a long way in easing our anxiety. Psychotherapists can help you to sort out stubborn dreads and get you asking the right questions.

Medications exist as well that can significantly reduce panic attacks and constant low-grade anxiety. These medications will not make stressful situations less stressful, but can make you more able to cope with these situations. If counseling alone has not helped reduce your fears, you may wish to consider starting a medication regime. Your primary care physician can prescribe medications if you and your therapist think they are worth a try. It can take as long as two months for some of them to kick in, however, so sooner is better than later.

Your depression is not who you are. It is a temporary disability. You have some control over it. It does not have to control you. While you are waiting for counseling or medication to start helping you, remember what Jesus said we should be doing instead of worrying. We need to strive for the kingdom. So befriend a person with a disability. Patch up an old quarrel. Volunteer with a local service agency or at church. When we have kingdom objectives on which to focus, we will not have to spend so much energy on not focusing on our anxieties.

Things to Think About

Why do so many people in this world not have their basic needs for food and clothing met? Is there anything you can do about it on even a very basic level?

Do you have some basic needs that are not being met? What would help you to meet these needs?

One way to address your fears is to ask yourself, "What's the worst thing that could possibly happen?" Think of an answer and then ask yourself, "So?" After you come up with a response, again ask yourself, "So?" For example, if you have a difficult relationship with a coworker, ask yourself, "What's the worst thing that ____ could do to me?" Answer: "She might make the supervisor angry at me." So? "My supervisor might fire me." So? "I wouldn't be able to pay the mortgage and we would lose the house." So? "My family would become homeless." So? And so on. Repeat this process until you have exhausted the possibilities.

How likely is it that your worst fears would be realized? If they were, how would you handle it? If a friend came to you and expressed fears of a similar nature, what would you tell him or her?

Prayer

God, I believe you will provide for my needs. Help me to focus on things of your kingdom instead of on my fears. Amen.

30

Hope outrageously

Luke 24:13-32

Now on that same day two of them were going to a village called Emmaus, about seven miles from Jerusalem, and talking with each other about all these things that had happened. While they were talking and discussing, Jesus himself came near and went with them, but their eyes were kept from recognizing him. And he said to them, "What are you discussing with each other while you walk along?" They stood still, looking sad. Then one of them, whose name was Cleopas, answered him, "Are you the only stranger in Jerusalem who does not know the things that have taken place there in these days?" He asked them, "What things?" They replied, "The things about Jesus of Nazareth, who was a prophet mighty in deed and word before God and all the people, and how our chief priests and leaders handed him over to be condemned to death and crucified him. But we had hoped that he was the one to redeem Israel. Yes, and besides all this, it is now the third day since these things took place. Moreover, some women of our group astounded us. They were at the tomb early this morning, and when they did not find his body there, they came back and told us that they had indeed seen a vision of angels who said that he was alive. Some of those who were with us went to the tomb and found it just as the women had said; but they did not see him." Then he said to them, "Oh, how foolish you are, and how slow of heart to believe all that the prophets have declared! Was it not necessary that the Messiah should suffer these things and then enter into his glory?" Then beginning with Moses and all the prophets, he interpreted to them the things about himself in all the scriptures. As they came near the village to which they were going, he walked ahead as if he were going on. But they urged him strongly, saying, "Stay with us, because it is almost evening and the day is now nearly over." So he went in to stay with them. When he was at the table with them, he took bread, blessed and broke it, and gave it to them. Then their eyes were opened, and they recognized him; and he vanished from their sight. They said to each other, "Were not our hearts burning within us while he was talking to us on the road, while he was opening the scriptures to us?"

The one who was to redeem Israel had died a death of slow torture. The Romans used crucifixion to show the conquered peoples what happened to traitors and subversives. They had crucified the teacher who had prophesied great things. They had crucified the man who many thought to be the Messiah.

How could any visitor to Jerusalem not have heard of the unjust condemnation of Jesus of Nazareth? The Jews, those who loved him and those who hated him, were talking of little else. In their grief, some of those who loved him had begun suffering delusions. Some crazy women had spoken of seeing angels at his tomb who had told them Jesus was alive. As much as they wanted to, Jesus' other followers could not bring themselves to believe it. But they had checked out the women's story–just in case. They had found nothing.

This visitor to Jerusalem became exasperated with them and showed them how the suffering and death of Jesus of Nazareth had been necessary in order that the prophecies of the Hebrew Bible might come true. Despite his rebuke, they asked him to stay with them that evening. In the breaking of the bread, their blindness came to an end, and they saw briefly that the stranger who taught them was Jesus himself. They should have known.

Application

I attended a chapel service at a Catholic college the week after Easter. In his homily, the priest said that Easter teaches us that we should not satisfy ourselves with puny hopes. Instead, we should dare to hope "outrageously." After his death, perhaps Jesus' followers hoped to live through the grief that was crushing them. Perhaps they hoped that the authorities would not come after them as they had come after Jesus. Perhaps it did not occur to them to hope that he had risen from the dead, even though they had heard the tales being spread by a bunch of women. And yet this hope, unlooked for, was fulfilled. Jesus came back to them, showing that the power of God was mightier than the whole of the Roman Empire.

We do not need merely to wish for cessation of pain. We can hope outrageously as well. We can hope for the restoration of broken relationships, for world peace, for justice to prevail. We can entertain the outrageous hope that someday we will feel joy again.

Another way to draw upon the Emmaus road story is to liken the blindness of Cleopas and his friend with the spiritual blindness we suffer as a result of our depression. Jesus walks with us all the time, but in our sadness we do not see him or feel his presence. Sometimes friends or therapists may tell us things about ourselves that we do not wish to see. They may force us to view personal deficits we would rather not acknowledge.

Like the two travelers on the Emmaus road, we need to invite these people to continue with us so that we might learn from them. The worst thing we can do is reject them or what they say out of hurt pride. We must have the humility and courage to face our deficits and accept help and advice. We too will someday feel the presence of Jesus, and the spell of our depression will be broken.

Things to Think About

Put yourself in the position of one of Jesus' followers in the days after his crucifixion. What things might you have hoped for? What would your reaction have been when the women first told you that Jesus' body was no longer in the tomb?

Can you think of some times during your spiritual journey when your heart has "burned within" you?

What in your mind constitutes a puny hope? An outrageous hope? What is the difference between a puny hope and a realistic hope?

What are some times when people have told you things that you did not want to hear but needed to hear? How did you react?

Can you think of some times when you have

been blind to Christ's presence in your life? How did that blindness end?

Prayer

God, give me the courage to hope outrageously. Open my eyes to your presence. Amen.

31

Shadows have no power

John 1:1-5

In the beginning was the Word, and the Word was with God, and the Word was God. He was in the beginning with God. All things came into being through him, and without him not one thing came into being. What has come into being in him was life, and the life was the light of all people. The light shines in the darkness, and the darkness did not overcome it.

One of my seminary professors pointed out that each of the Gospels has a progressively greater scope. Mark begins with Jesus' ministry. Matthew begins with Jesus' birth. Luke begins with the period before Jesus' conception. John begins at the beginning of time. The hymnlike words that open the Gospel of John consciously recall the first words of the Book of Genesis. Before the beginning, before creation, God existed and Christ existed with God.

The Greek text of this passage can bewilder the reader. So much is compacted into so few verses: light and darkness, creation, reality, the nature of God, the nature of Christ, the nature of the "logos" (word). From the time this gospel achieved widespread circulation, serious students of the Bible have debated the exact meaning of John's use of "logos." Dozens of nuances have been woven into these mystical and powerful words.

For our own purposes, we will focus on John's conception of reality and his comparison of light and darkness. John connects these concepts, saying that all reality, all creation, has to do with God's efforts. Life and light are a part of this reality.

In *A Commentary on the Gospel According to John* (Hendrickson, 1968), Dorothy G. Sanders and B. A. Mastin suggest that the logical extension of this thought is that anything not connected with God has a "spurious reality." In other words, the darkness–the forces antithetical to God–are but shadows with no real power in and of themselves. A tree may cast a shadow when the sun shines upon it, but on a cloudy night, that shadow ceases to exist. Darkness is merely the absence of light.

The word translated by the New Revised Standard Version as "overcome" has several meanings. The King James Version's use of "comprehend" comes closest to matching it. "Comprehend" can mean both "to understand" and "to encompass, include, or cover." The latter meaning is more old-fashioned. In Edward Gibbon's *The History of the Decline and Fall of the Roman Empire*, published in the eighteenth century, the opening paragraph uses the word in that sense: "In the second century of the Christian Era, the empire of Rome comprehended the fairest part of the earth and the most civilized portion of mankind" (p. 1).

For centuries people have debated which

meaning John intended, but it is possible that he intended both. The darkness, having no reality, has no powers of understanding or comprehension. Its lack of reality also makes it impossible for it to overcome the light, for its only reality is that of "un-light." Its shadow existence is but a by-product of the light.

These words may have held great comfort for the Christians in Rome when Nero began persecuting them. (Some speculate that the Gospel of John achieved written form around this time–64 C.E.) The author of the Gospel wanted believers to understand that the forces of darkness had only temporary power over them. They had no hope of prevailing against the power of the light. Even if the darkness caused the Christians to die for their faith, they would understand–once they stood in the reality of God's kingdom–that what they thought was real in this world was just a shadow. In God's presence they would see reality for the first time.

Application

Christians in North America do not often face persecution for their beliefs, certainly not to the extremes the Christians faced under Nero. However, as part of a fallen humanity we suffer, and these words can speak to our emotional sufferings as well.

Sometimes it helps to acknowledge that our depression and anxiety have a "spurious reality." They are a part of the shadow world we live in. This does not mean that the pain does not hurt us or affect our lives, but we need to remember that someday we will stand in the light of God's presence. We will see how insubstantial these sufferings look beside joy so intense that we could not have felt it while we lived in the shadow world. Like bad dreams that fade away moments after waking, so will human pain fade away into nothing when we stand before God's throne.

Things to Think About

Where are you right now? On what are you sitting, lying, or standing? Whom do you love? Where is God in your life? How do these things seem real to you? Now think of the aspects of your life that make you most fearful and anxious. Do they seem more or less real to you than your surroundings and emotional attachments?

What constitutes the "forces of darkness" to you? How much power do they wield in this world?

How can you both acknowledge the realities of human suffering in an effort to alleviate it, and regard it as a temporary aberration from God's perfection?

Prayer

God, your reality is beyond what I can imagine. Help me to understand my pain as temporary. Give me the strength to endure it until I stand within your complete reality, and my pain is no more. Amen.

32

Act courageously

John 11:1-16

Now a certain man was ill, Lazarus of Bethany, the village of Mary and her sister Martha. Mary was the one who anointed the Lord with perfume and wiped his feet with her hair; her brother Lazarus was ill. So the sisters sent a message to Jesus, "Lord, he whom you love is ill." But when Jesus heard it, he said, "This illness does not lead to death; rather it is for God's glory, so that the Son of God may be glorified through it." Accordingly, though Jesus loved Martha and her sister and Lazarus, after having heard that Lazarus was ill, he stayed two days longer in the place where he was. Then after this he said to the disciples, "Let us go to Judea again." The disciples said to him, "Rabbi, the Jews were just now trying to stone you, and are you going there again?" Jesus answered, "Are there not twelve hours of daylight? Those who walk during the day do not stumble, because they see the light of this world. But those who walk at night stumble, because the light is not in them." After saying this, he told them, "Our friend Lazarus has fallen asleep, but I am going there to awaken him." The disciples said to him, "Lord, if he has fallen asleep, he will be all right." Jesus, however, had been speaking about his death, but they thought that he was referring merely to sleep. Then Jesus told them plainly, "Lazarus is dead. For your sake I am glad I was not there, so that you may believe. But let us go to him." Thomas, who was called the Twin, said to his fellow disciples, "Let us also go, that we may die with him."

We do not usually remember the story of Lazarus's resurrection for the insight it gives us into the character of Thomas. Yet the story speaks to the place of doubt in the spiritual journey of the believer.

We remember this disciple as the "Doubting Thomas" of John 20:19-29 who would not believe the reports of the other disciples. Thomas insisted that he would have to physically touch Jesus' wounds before he would believe Jesus was alive.

In John 11, the disciples misunderstood Jesus. He told them that they would see God's glory reflected in his healing of Lazarus. But the disciples, mindful that Jesus' enemies wished to kill him, encouraged Jesus not to go. Since Jesus had already told them that at stake is the revelation of Jesus as the Son of God, he expected them to understand that he spoke euphemistically about waking Lazarus from sleep. One did not have to be the Son of God to wake someone up, of course. Characteristically, the disciples didn't get it, and Jesus finally had to spell it out for them.

Thomas was as dense as the rest of the disciples, but his loyalty to Jesus was greater than his fear of what could happen. He might not have thought that Jesus had chosen a sensible course. He might not have wanted to risk his life. But if Jesus persisted in following a course that might lead to his death, Thomas wanted to be there and die with him.

This one sentence of Thomas enlarges the kingdom of God to include those people who feel at times they have a shaky faith. There are many for whom issues like the divinity of Christ, the goodness of God, and the power of God to intervene in everyday life loom as insurmountable obstacles. Some days these people cannot believe in these things even though they want very much to believe in them. Thomas provides a route for these people to follow Jesus. Even if they do not have the perfect faith they desire, they can still make the decision to follow Jesus, sometimes to their own death. They may not fully believe in what they should believe in, but they can choose to die for these beliefs.

Application

Depression can often cause crises of faith–and sometimes crises of faith can cause depression. We cannot force ourselves to believe what we want to believe in, but we can choose to act courageously. Like Thomas, we can choose to act in the cause of Christ even when we doubt our faith in Christ.

The parable of the wise and foolish house builders (Matthew 7:24-27) also speaks to the issue of faith. Notice that Jesus did not tell his listeners what materials these men built their houses out of. What mattered was the foundation upon which the men built. A mansion of stone built upon the sand would fall in the event of a flood, but a crooked hovel built upon the rock of God's word would remain secure. Our own faith does not have to be perfect, as long as it is grounded in God.

On a personal level, we can carry these thoughts into how we behave when depressed.

We may desire to stay in bed all day and not face the world. When we do make the effort to get up, get dressed, and function as a normal person, we are making a statement of faith. We may still feel miserable and anxious, but when we carry on in spite of these feelings, we not only promote our healing, we fulfill God's expectations of us.

Things to Think About

Has your depression affected your faith in Christ? If so, how? If not, how have you managed to detach your faith from your emotional condition? Is it possible to channel some of the strength of your faith into your emotional condition?

Make a list of the beliefs you do not feel certain of but for which you are willing to die.

If you could characterize your faith as a type of building, what would it look like? What are some ways you can make such a structure, grounded on God's word, stronger?

Have you ever met someone with perfect faith or with a faith much stronger than your own? How did it affect that person's personality? Have you ever known someone whose faith you thought was stronger than your own but who subsequently stopped believing?

What is the difference between perfect faith and fanaticism?

Prayer

God, my faith may be shaky and insubstantial, but you are real and strong. Give me the courage to live as you would have me live, and to die as you would have me die. Amen.

33

Learning to feel joy again

Romans 5:1-8

Therefore, since we are justified by faith, we have peace with God through our Lord Jesus Christ, through whom we have obtained access to this grace in which we stand; and we boast in our hope of sharing the glory of God. And not only that, but we also boast in our sufferings, knowing that suffering produces endurance, and endurance produces character, and character produces hope, and hope does not disappoint us, because God's love has been poured into our hearts through the Holy Spirit that has been given to us. For while we were still weak, at the right time Christ died for the ungodly. Indeed, rarely will anyone die for a righteous person—though perhaps for a good person someone might actually dare to die. But God proves his love for us in that while we still were sinners Christ died for us.

Some scholars believe that Romans 5–8 is the most important section of his letter to the Romans, and possibly of all his letters. It follows an explanation of justification by faith and explains what the implications of this justification are for the lives of believers.

Verses 3 and 4, which are of most concern to

us, should have parentheses around them, for they interrupt the thought begun in verse 2 that picks up again in verse 5. Paul, who wrote of the joy and peace available to believers, remembered that he and his fellow believers suffered greatly for their faith. The connection is clear between this suffering and the "hope of sharing the glory of God" as mentioned in verse 2.

Paul said that the sufferings of Christians produce hope. When they learn to bear their sufferings patiently, they strengthen their endurance. Endurance acts as a character builder, and when people have developed a strong character, they naturally develop hope.

Of course, the true source of our hope as Christians is the "grace in which we stand." Paul, however, wanted to demonstrate that far from causing Christians to lose hope, grace gives them access to the hope that is theirs through justification by faith.

Unlike the hopes and dreams of human fantasy, the hope we have in Christ Jesus will not let us down or prove to be an illusion. The hardships we suffer here on earth will seem of no account when we face our fulfilled hope in heaven. How do we know that our hope for heaven is not an illusion? Because God has demonstrated love for us in the death of Jesus. That love shows us that God wants us to be with God.

Application

Suffering does not always build character. It can make people bitter and twisted inside. Some people, having experienced hunger or poverty, become stingy and unwilling to share even from their abundance. Other people who have gone through the same experience will remember what it felt like to be hungry and poor every time they see a person in need and will want to reach out to that person.

As Christians we must choose the latter response to suffering. Depression can make us self-absorbed and weak. In fact, we may feel self-absorbed and weak even when we fight it and choose to continue functioning. And choose to fight we must. Sometimes that may mean getting out of bed instead of staying in it for the day. It might mean doing a favor for someone instead of withdrawing into a world of television or books. It means seeking help for the depression when it begins to affect our ability to function.

Conquering depression and remaining the same person we were before is impossible. Our character will be stronger. We will know that we have some control over how we feel. We will know what we have to do in order to heal. We will know that we can endure another bout of depression, because we did so before. Because we healed once before, we have the hope for healing again.

Once we find our ability to feel joy again, we may wish to ask ourselves, "How can I use my depression for the glory of God?" A logical response would be to find someone else who is suffering and tell them that you know there is hope.

Things to Think About

Has the suffering you have experienced in your life made you weaker or stronger? How might you have turned out if you had become weaker instead of stronger, or stronger instead of weaker?

Define "character." What is a "person of character" like?

What is the church's response to people who suffer? What is society's response?

What are some hopes you have had that were never fulfilled?

Think of people you know who have suffered. Which ones would you like to emulate? Why?

Prayer

God, help me use my pain to become a better servant of your kingdom. Amen.

34

New life from old pain

Romans 8:14-23

For all who are led by the Spirit of God are children of God. For you did not receive a spirit of slavery to fall back into fear, but you have received a spirit of adoption. When we cry, "Abba! Father!" it is that very Spirit bearing witness with our spirit that we are children of God, and if children, then heirs, heirs of God and joint heirs with Christ–if, in fact, we suffer with him so that we may also be glorified with him. I consider that the sufferings of this present time are not worth comparing with the glory about to be revealed to us. For the creation waits with eager longing for the revealing of the children of God; for the creation was subjected to futility, not of its own will but by the will of the one who subjected it, in hope that the creation itself will be set free from its bondage to decay and will obtain the freedom of the glory of the children of God. We know that the whole creation has been groaning in labor pains until now; and not only the creation, but we ourselves, who have the first fruits of the Spirit, groan inwardly while we wait for adoption, the redemption of our bodies.

In this passage Paul returned to the theme of hope–hope based on the Christians' status as children of God. He told his readers that the fact they suffered as Christ did establishes their legitimacy as heirs to the kingdom. He then went into a sort of sidebar on the subject of suffering, seeing it as the natural state of all creation.

Jewish thought of this period commonly viewed Adam's fall as tainting all of creation. Some apocalyptic and apocryphal literature focused on the restoration of nature as a part of the result of the coming of the Messiah. Often these writers viewed nature only in terms of the material abundance it would provide to the faithful.

Paul, however, showed a surprising compassion for nature for its own sake–surprising because Paul did not often use nature metaphors in his writings, preferring the terminology of the military and athletic competitions.

In this passage, Paul personified creation. Creation will have a shot at redemption when God's children receive their divine inheritance. So creation waits for this moment eagerly. Paul interpreted Genesis 3:17 to mean that God had subjected all of creation to a futile existence. Nature had been forced to live in an endless cycle of seasons and decay. Strong animals attacked the weaker ones. Erosion and entropy took their course. Fires, floods, and earthquakes added to its torments.

Paul's pregnancy metaphor seems especially appropriate when describing what creation must endure. Pregnancy can be the most dangerous event in a woman's life. Delivery and birth are certainly one of the most painful things that any woman can endure. Women can literally be in labor for days. When the wrenching pain is over, however, the child which has come into the world claims the love of his or her parents, and the pain swiftly fades.

Paul encouraged believers in their sufferings by letting them know that all of creation suffers with them. The outcome of all the pain for humankind and creation is new life.

Application

"And there's not enough room in this world for my pain" is a line in the song "Ghost" written by Emily Saliers (*Rites of Passage*, Sony, 1992). In this song Saliers describes how the memories of a lost love haunt her until she can feel little else than pain.

Those of us who have lost loved ones and feel crippled by our grief can empathize with Saliers' words. We may feel that we cannot contain the grief inside us. Its expanse touches every corner of the known universe. Every sunny day, every crisp wind, every mountain, lake, or river–all that once brought us joy seems polluted by our negative emotions. Nothing we used to value seems to help us. Even fellowship with those we respect and love does not soothe the dull, insistent ache in our chests. Though friends and family surround us, we still feel alone.

Helpful people may encourage us to put our depression into perspective, but that can precisely be the last thing a suffering person should do. We can feel overwhelmed by the poverty, war, and famine in the world. Instead of making our own problems seem small by comparison, it can make us feel that no place in the world remains untouched by despair. We can get to the point when global tragedies seem to make more sense to us than any acts of kindness or heroism.

Even on a personal level, it can be dangerous to compare your misery to other peoples' more "important" miseries. When we see people we care about suffering from disease or looking for a job, instead of viewing ourselves as fortunate, we can think, "Gee, if I'm barely getting by with my problems, I don't understand how they can keep on living. I'd kill myself if I felt any worse than I do now."

Anything that keeps us from fully functioning as servants of God's kingdom needs to be dealt with. God works through the lives of believers to bring healing to our sadly troubled world. Working with a counselor can help you to focus on the problems you need to deal with before you can function as an instrument of God. When you feel strong enough to handle your own problems, then you can put them into perspective of human suffering. And maybe, having dealt with your own sadness, you can help others to deal with theirs. In your healing and their healing, new lives will emerge.

Things to Think About

Define "heir." How does this definition apply to our relationship with God?

Does viewing God as a parent arouse negative or positive emotions within you? How does your relationship with your parents affect your relationship with God?

Do you view nature as a hostile or as a sympathetic force? What are some of the ways in which creation suffers?

Have there been times in your life when

putting your situation into perspective helped you? Have there been times when it didn't help?

What do you view as the most important problems in the world today? Is there any way that you can address these problems?

Prayer

God, I feel sometimes that despair is the natural order of things. Give me the strength to change so that I can more fully function as a servant of your kingdom. Amen.

35

Secure in God's love

Romans 8:26-39

Likewise the Spirit helps us in our weakness; for we do not know how to pray as we ought, but that very Spirit intercedes with sighs too deep for words. And God, who searches the heart, knows what is the mind of the Spirit, because the Spirit intercedes for the saints according to the will of God. We know that all things work together for good for those who love God, who are called according to his purpose. For those whom he foreknew he also predestined to be conformed to the image of his Son, in order that he might be the firstborn within a large family. And those whom he predestined he also called; and those whom he called he also justified; and those whom he justified he also glorified. What then are we to say about these things? If God is for us, who is against us? He who did not withhold his own Son, but gave him up for all of us, will he not with him also give us everything else? Who will bring any charge against God's elect? It is God who justifies. Who is to condemn? It is Christ Jesus, who died, yes, who was raised, who is at the right hand of God, who indeed intercedes for us. Who will separate us from the love of Christ? Will hardship, or distress, or persecution, or famine, or nakedness, or peril, or sword? As it is written, "For your sake we are being killed all day long;

we are accounted as sheep to be slaughtered." No, in all these things we are more than conquerors through him who loved us. For I am convinced that neither death, nor life, nor angels, nor rulers, nor things present, nor things to come, nor powers, nor height, nor depth, nor anything else in all creation, will be able to separate us from the love of God in Christ Jesus our Lord.

Four ideas from Romans 8:26-39 stand out when thinking about dealing with depression.

1. The Holy Spirit intercedes with us in "sighs too deep for words." Sometimes there are no words in any human language to describe our suffering. A more literal translation of the first part of verse 26 is "We do not know what to pray as is necessary." Paul assured his readers that God, aware of our human weakness, sent the Holy Spirit to work within us and to say what needs to be said.

A parent helping a child learn to read or write does not criticize the child's illegible scrawls. Instead, the parent helps the child learn to write more clearly, assisting him or her in finding the words the child needs to communicate. Likewise, the Holy Spirit provides the means by which we can communicate with God.

2. "All things work together for good for those who love God." God may not cause human tragedies, but God can work through them to make a positive outcome. Indeed, God can make an outcome more positive than if the tragedy had never occurred. Paul told his readers that God would do just that with the sufferings they must endure.

In keeping with his teachings on justification and predestination, Paul modified "those who love God" with those "who are called according to his purpose." The love we have for God does not give us "brownie points." In fact, it is not a love we initiate at all but a natural response to God's love for us.

3. "If God is for us, who is against us?" Paul liked to ask rhetorical questions. The fact that God let Jesus–God's own son–die for us proves that God's love for us stands strong. Both Paul and his followers could have probably listed a number of enemies who stood against them.

However, Paul maintained that the rejection of family and friends and persecution by the authorities do not really amount to much when seen in the light of God's solidarity with us.

4. "Nothing can separate us from the love of Christ." At the time Paul wrote the letter to the Romans, Christians had not yet experienced the empire-wide persecutions ordained by the Roman emperors. However, local persecutions by religious leaders and Roman prefects did sometimes affect them. We should also consider the suffering of Christians when their families rejected them.

Paul knew that he and his followers lived in dangerous times. In seeking to give them courage, he told them human evil did not have any power to permanently harm them. In fact, the cosmic forces of death, life, and time itself had no power to separate them from God's love through Jesus Christ. Even if the forces of evil kill them, they could rest in the confidence that then they would stand in God's presence, filled with a joy far beyond their power to imagine.

Application

Romans 8:26-39 blazes with hope for people suffering from depression. Sometimes when our despair overwhelms us, we find it impossible to believe that our prayers can penetrate the force field of anxiety and sadness that encloses us. Sometimes we cannot find the words to emphasize strongly our need for God's help. We need to have the faith that God does hear our prayers, even when all we can do is repeat "Jesus, Jesus" over and over again. Our depressed emotions are no match for the Holy Spirit, which works within us to break up the force field. The Holy Spirit will create the right words.

The Holy Spirit will also work within us as we struggle with the daily miseries of life. The question of whether God causes tragedies or allows them to happen has troubled believers for centuries. Whether or not we believe God causes tragedies, we can certainly believe that God works through tragedies to make us better servants of the divine kingdom. Every time we are afflicted and healed, we become a bit wiser, a bit stronger, and a bit more able to respond fully to God's love.

The phrase "If God is for us, who can be against us" can be misused by people afflicted with paranoia. These people think everyone they know is out to get them. Many also believe that God alone is on their side. These people sometimes turn out to be leaders of cults or loners who unexpectedly turn up at work one day with a subautomatic weapon.

For those of us not given to that degree of

paranoia, we may find deep comfort in these words. We may not have enemies, as such, but most of us have experienced unhelpful criticism from parents or experienced coworkers stabbing us in the back in order to get ahead. When we reflect that these injustices do not mean a whole lot when placed beside the power of God, we can break out of our self-pity. We can forgive the people who hurt us, because those hurts just don't affect God's love and protection of us.

Finally, when we realize that none of the hurts laid upon us or brought upon ourselves can make a difference in Christ's love for us, we can feel great hope. If "neither death, nor life, nor angels, nor rulers, nor things present, nor things to come, nor powers, nor height, nor depth, nor anything else in all creation" is able to separate us from the love of God in Christ Jesus, our depression doesn't stand a chance.

Things to Think About

Have there been times in your life when you had difficulty communicating with God? Did anything happen to change that?

How has God worked through the difficult times in your life to create a positive outcome? How has God worked through other people's lives?

Do you have enemies? Who are they? How have they interfered with your relationship to God? Do you pray for them?

Are there people who simply rub you the wrong way? How do you react to them? Do you pray for them?

Have there been times when you felt utterly separated from God?

Prayer

God, I believe your love for me is stronger than all of human evil and all of the forces of the universe combined. Give me the faith to believe in that love and to show it to others. Amen.

36

Love for today

1 Corinthians 13:8-13

Love never ends. But as for prophecies, they will come to an end; as for tongues, they will cease; as for knowledge, it will come to an end. For we know only in part, and we prophesy only in part; but when the complete comes, the partial will come to an end. When I was a child, I spoke like a child, I thought like a child, I reasoned like a child; when I became an adult, I put an end to childish ways. For now we see in a mirror, dimly, but then we will see face to face. Now I know only in part; then I will know fully, even as I have been fully known. And now faith, hope, and love abide, these three; and the greatest of these is love.

Paul expressed several complex ideas in this passage. The common thread that binds them is a contrast between the imperfect present and the perfect–as yet unrealized–future.

Love belongs to this unrealized time. It also belongs to our imperfect present, giving us a faint reflection of the divine love we will experience fully in the next age.

Note that Paul does not speak of the partial as gradually growing until it becomes complete. Rather, this partial world–this shadow world–will come to an end, abruptly, when the reality of God's kingdom appears.

In verse 12 Paul makes an allusion to Numbers 12:6-8. In this passage, Moses' sister Miriam and brother Aaron criticized Moses for marrying an Ethiopian woman. God had come down in a pillar of fire to speak to them:

> And he said, "Hear my words:
> When there are prophets among you,
> I the Lord make myself known
> to them in visions;
> I speak to them in dreams.
> Not so with my servant Moses;
> He is entrusted with all my house.
> With him I speak face to face–clearly,
> not in riddles;
> And he beholds the form of the Lord."

The Greek version of what we call the Old Testament is called the Septuagint. When Paul quoted from Scripture, he used the Septuagint. The Greek word in 1 Corinthians 13:12 that is translated in the New Revised Standard Version as "dimly," is the same Greek root word in Numbers 12:8 that is translated as "riddles." It is the root word from which we derive the English word "enigma."

At the time Paul wrote these words, mirrors were made of polished metal and did not give the clear reflection that present-day mirrors do. Paul tied the image of an indistinct reflection with the passage from Numbers to emphasize our inability to understand fully God's plan for us. As imperfect human beings, we have to find the solution to the riddle of this plan. As in the game of Twenty Questions, some guesses give us clues to this solution and some lead us off track.

The frustrating search for the answer to the riddle will pay off, though. Some day God will speak to us as clearly as God spoke to Moses. Some day we will know God as fully as God knows us. The love we know here on earth is but a reflection of the love we will know in heaven. But this love is still our best clue to understanding what is to come.

Application

Someone once said that most people, if given a choice, would choose the certainty of misery over the misery of uncertainty. Anyone suffering from depression understands this truth. We are told that prayer, medication, and counseling will probably help us. We just have to wait for their effects.

"How long?" we ask. Even to be told that our depression will last for exactly two years, exiting promptly on New Year's Eve, would make the whole thing seem easier. We could bear the suffering better if we knew its dimensions.

If someone told us we had to carry a hundred-pound weight for a hundred miles, we would know that it would take a long time. We know we would strain our backs along the way, but we also would know that the journey had an end.

Depression is like being handed the burden with no instructions. We ask how heavy it is, how far we must carry it, and receive no answers. We carry it up and down hill, through swamps and deserts, never knowing if this is the last hill or swamp or whether we have a hundred more to go. Some people might decide that sitting in the swamp is preferable to trekking on. Some may choose to die rather than to continue.

As servants of the risen Lord, we have no choice but to continue. We need to know, however, that it is okay not to know how the future will turn out. No one really does know, after all. We who have experienced God's love do have a clue to the riddle of our sometimes dreary existence. We know that God loves us–so much that God sent Jesus to suffer with us. A day will come when we understand what this love means and why we had to make that journey we thought would never end.

Things to Think About

What are some times you have chosen the certainty of misery over the misery of uncertainty (and vice versa)?

What is it about the future that scares you most? What hopes for the future give you the most comfort?

What are some times you have felt God's love, either directly or through other human beings?

Prayer

God, give me strength to carry my burdens and the strength to believe that this long journey has an ending. Help me to focus on the present reality of your love instead of my fear of the future. Amen.

37

Rely on others

2 Corinthians 1:8-11

We do not want you to be unaware, brothers and sisters, of the affliction we experienced in Asia; for we were so utterly, unbearably crushed that we despaired of life itself. Indeed, we felt that we had received the sentence of death so that we would rely not on ourselves but on God who raises the dead. He who rescued us from so deadly a peril will continue to rescue us; on him we have set our hope that he will rescue us again, as you also join in helping us by your prayers, so that many will give thanks on our behalf for the blessing granted us through the prayers of many.

We do not know the danger of which Paul wrote in this passage. He had just spoken to the Corinthians about the sufferings of Christ and the suffering that Christians share in general. The fact that he gave few details could indicate that the Corinthians might already have known about Paul's sufferings in Asia (a Roman province in Western Asia Minor). Paul's mentioning it here might indicate that the Corinthians had not known the severity of his sufferings.

The situation in 2 Corinthians 1 must have

been incredibly severe if it drove Paul to despair. Paul certainly felt he had met his death, but through some miraculous intervention, God delivered him and his companions.

As with everything else, Paul saw God's hand in the making of this time of despair. Paul, a man of strong character, had managed capably in his ministry, facing any number of disasters. He told the Corinthians that he had become too self-reliant, and that whatever happened to him in Asia had served to make him realize that he should rely on God alone. Paul may have had two thoughts in mind when he referred to God as one "who raises from the dead." God had miraculously delivered Paul and his people from certain death, which in and of itself is a type of resurrection. Secondly, Paul may have had in mind that in the event that death should come to him and his readers, God, the only true author of life and death, would be in control. They need not fear death.

We expect Paul to find some hope in any situation. Sure enough, in verse 10 he rebounded from the "utterly, unbearably crushed" status he had suffered to that of a man confident in God's ability to protect and preserve him. Paul expected to find himself in peril again at some point, perhaps even to the point of death, but his hope in God's deliverance rests secure.

Paul closed this section by telling the Corinthians what part their prayers have played and will play in his ministry. The Greek of this sentence is rather involved, but the meaning seems to be that the Corinthians should pray for Paul when future crises occur. When God answers their prayers, Paul's subsequent deliverance will lead many other people to praise God.

Application

Sometimes the worst words someone who is depressed can hear are phrases like "Don't give up hope," "Keep your chin up," or "Look on the bright side."

We want to cry, "We would hope if we could. Do you think we choose to live without hope?"

Fortunately, as Paul noted in this passage, we do not have to rely on our own hope to give us comfort. God, of course, is a God of hope and God imparts hope to others. Sometimes, when we feel hopeless about our situation, we can look to the hope of others. Indeed, looking to others for help is a sign of humility. Paul noted that realizing he could not rely on himself was a turning point in his spiritual journey. When we have friends and family who have the conviction that things will get better, we can choose to lean on that hope. Knowing that someone else has hope for us can bring a much-needed sense of security.

We can even look to Paul to share vicariously in his hope. Paul knew what it felt like to be hopeless. He had come to a situation in which he felt "so utterly and unbearably crushed" that he "despaired of life itself." This was the same man who wrote, "We know that all things work together for good for those who love God." Although Paul wrote much on the topic of hope, he was not a blind optimist. He had faced torments of the body and torments of the soul. Knowing that Paul hoped in the face of adversity can inspire us to do likewise. And if we cannot feel hope, we can hope vicariously through Paul. He probably would have been happy to help.

Things to Think About

Can you think of some times in your life when you felt "utterly and unbearably crushed?" What was the outcome?

Which would you prefer to deal with, physical danger or depression? How are the two similar? How are they different?

Can you think of times when you have been inspired by a story of someone escaping peril? How do stories like these affect your relationship with God?

Do you prefer the company of optimists or pessimists? How would you classify yourself? What functions in a relationship do both types of people serve?

Have there been times in your life when it helped to have someone tell you that everything was going to turn out all right? Who are the people you can count on to say this with conviction?

Prayer

God, you are a God of hope. Thank you for giving that hope to people. Give me the humility to borrow the hope of others when I cannot find it within myself. Amen.

38

God does care

1 Peter 5:7-11

Cast all your anxiety on him, because he cares for you. Discipline yourselves, keep alert. Like a roaring lion your adversary the devil prowls around, looking for someone to devour. Resist him, steadfast in your faith, for you know that your brothers and sisters in all the world are undergoing the same kinds of suffering. And after you have suffered for a little while, the God of all grace, who has called you to his eternal glory in Christ, will himself restore, support, strengthen, and establish you. To him be the power forever and ever. Amen.

The book of 1 Peter is one of those little books at the back of the Bible that you can miss when riffling through to get to Revelation. Nevertheless, it contains one of the most important theological statements in all of the sixty-six books of the Bible.

While the concept of a compassionate God who cared for God's children was not foreign to the Jews, it would have seemed strange to many people who worshiped the gods of the Greeks, Romans, and Mesopotamian countries. The theology surrounding many of these deities consisted of the idea that a god might deign to show favor to mortals, if these mortals stroked its ego by offering sacrifices. The simple words "God cares for you" would have had an enormous impact on Gentile Christians unfamiliar with Israel's God.

Entrusting God with our anxieties does not mean we should act without caution. The words translated by the New Revised Standard Version as "discipline yourselves" are the same as those that Jesus spoke to his disciples in the Garden of Gethsemane when he tells them "Keep awake." The readers of this letter had many enemies–those who persecuted them, and even the devil–who might tempt them away from their commitment to God.

These early Christians could take some comfort in the knowledge that members of the fledgling church throughout the Roman Empire were undergoing the same sorts of trials. They also knew that their sufferings would not last forever. The word translated by the NRSV as "restore" appears also in Mark 1:19 to refer to the mending of nets. Greek literature outside of the Bible uses the word to refer to the setting of broken bones. Though their sufferings might "break" them, Christians could look forward to a time when God would mend all their hurts and create for them a place where the hurts of the world could not touch them.

Application

I teach a Red Cross cardiopulmonary resuscitation course in which, in addition to CPR, I teach rescue breathing and what to do when someone is choking.

Of these three techniques, the one used to alleviate choking is the most complicated. It calls for the rescuer to make more decisions than do the regular patterns of rescue breathing and CPR. Frequently, students ask me why they don't check the pulse of an unconscious person with an airway obstruction. I tell them there is no point in doing so. Until they clear the airway obstruction, they can do nothing else for the victim. The best CPR techniques in the world can do nothing for a victim if the rescuer cannot get air through to the victim's lungs. The first step is to get rid of the blockage in the airway.

First Peter 5:7 contains a spiritual truth so basic that all other theology is in vain until believers accept its truth. If we do not believe that God cares about us, why bother discussing methods of biblical interpretation or theological concepts like predestination or the Trinity? Paul's commentary on the importance of love in 1 Corinthians 13 holds true in this case as well. If we do not believe that God loves us, we can do nothing to access God's healing power or come closer to spiritual enlightenment.

What do we do then when we cannot feel God's love? when we have doubts whether God does in fact love us?

Remember that in human relationships, we do not always feel the love others might have for us. Parents may become too preoccupied with worldly concerns to show us the love we need, but when a crisis arises, we can find ourselves enveloped by their raging maternal and paternal instincts.

Brothers and sisters who tortured us physically and mentally as children can turn out to be our best friends when we grow up. The love was always there. Sin just got in the way of our seeing it.

As with hope, we can participate vicariously in the conviction that God loves us by looking to others who do feel it. When the knowledge of God's love possesses a person, that person provides a sturdy structure to lean against when we feel weak. Relying on other people stronger than ourselves is a sign of humility–a quality which God heartily endorses. When belief in God's love for us possesses us as well, we can then stand on our own and begin to heal.

Things to Think About

Why is the conviction that God loves us basic to our faith? Think of some of the other spiritual beliefs you have about God, Jesus, the Holy Spirit, the Bible, etc. How does each of these beliefs relate to God's love for us?

What gets in the way of casting our anxiety on God? What are some ways we can deal with these obstructions?

Does it help or aggravate your depression to think of other people going through similar experiences?

What are some areas in your life you need God's help in mending?

Prayer

God, I believe that you love me. I love you, too. Help me to show your love to others. Amen.

39

Letting go of guilt

James 4:7-10

Submit yourselves therefore to God. Resist the devil, and he will flee from you. Draw near to God, and he will draw near to you. Cleanse your hands, you sinners, and purify your hearts, you double-minded. Lament and mourn and weep. Let your laughter be turned into mourning and your joy into dejection. Humble yourselves before the Lord, and he will exalt you.

Martin Luther called the New Testament book James "an epistle of straw." Having developed his theology from Paul that salvation comes from grace rather than works, it annoyed him to read in James 2:14, "What good is it, my brothers and sisters, if you say you have faith but do not have works? Can faith save you?"

As it happened, a book of ethical instructions for the new church was necessary, especially for Gentile Christians who had not received the morally rigorous training of Jewish Christians. Paul, in his letters, instructed Christians on their behavior, and the writer of James may very well have borrowed material from Paul's letters. The entire purpose of James seems to be to set standards of Christian behavior.

The selected text belongs within a larger section (4:1-10) that deals with sinful desires Christians might have. In telling his followers to resist the devil, the writer referred specifically to sinful desires. If Christians resist temptation, then temptation will not bother them. The image of a schoolyard bully comes to mind. When children allow themselves to be cowed by the bully, he or she will torment them more relentlessly. A mere act of defiance or resistance–even nonviolent resistance–may be enough to stop the bully from future harassment.

The reference to the cleansing of hands could be meant on both a ritualistic and moral level. Observant Jews washed their hands as a part of a ritual before eating. However, the writer of James also probably meant that Christians should cease committing impure actions. They cannot both serve the world and follow earthly pleasures and serve God.

James did not tell his readers that they should wear sackcloth and sit in ashes when he said to "lament and mourn and weep." Rather, he wanted them to stop following the "cheap thrills" of the world. It is far better to weep than to join in on raucous laughter at a perverted joke. It is better to feel dejected than transported with joy over a new possession. When his followers find the true humility of Christ's servants, they will view their pleasures in things of the world as horror.

Application

In a sense, this passage from James may not seem applicable to the struggles of a depressed person.

After all, when one suffers depression, one is basically unable to take pleasure in either the pleasures of this world or the pleasures of the Spirit. Far from being double-minded as the text indicates, we may feel non-minded. We do not feel inclined to take part in cheap thrills or deeply meaningful spiritual encounters. We just want to sleep, or cocoon ourselves into a narcotic stupor in front of the TV.

Where depression connects with the passage is on the subject of sin and the subsequent guilt, which as the writer indicates, manifests itself in mourning and dejection.

There is a time and a place for guilt. If guilt brings repentance and thus draws us closer to God, then we can think of it as a positive emotion. Guilt does not always lead to repentance, however. I once heard a pastor say in a sermon that teaching people to feel responsible empowers them, but making them feel guilty immobilizes them.

Depression feeds on guilt and guilt feeds on depression. In order for us to become truly healed, we must use our guilt only in its function as a promoter of responsibility. We need to assess how we have harmed people and what we can do about it. If we have hurt people and sinned against God, we need to "lament and mourn and weep." In fact, it would be inappropriate if we did not do so.

There comes a time, however, when mourning for our sins must end if we expect to get on with the healing process. Obsessing on our moral failures is another little self-destructive game that depression encourages. If we can do nothing to compensate for a sin we have committed in the past, and if we have asked God to forgive us for that sin, we need to let it go. We have no right to continue punishing ourselves if God has forgiven us. If we can do something to atone for hurts we may have inflicted on others, we should do so immediately. It will be one less obstacle in our way towards spiritual healing. We can choose, of course, to keep the obstacle. But in doing so, we stubbornly hold on to a sin that God has already forgiven.

We have all sinned and fallen short of the glory of God. Depressed and happy people, mentally well and mentally ill people all need to repent and be forgiven. That repentance may include lamenting, mourning, and weeping. Mourning continued beyond that point, however, is self-indulgence. We should get rid of it.

Things to Think About

Make a list of all the people you can remember hurting in your life. Have you attempted to ask forgiveness of any of them? Have you asked God to forgive you? If you have done what you can to restore right relationships, burn the list.

Make a list of the ways in which you abuse yourself. Do you intend to stop? Have you asked God to forgive you for your self-destructive behavior? If so, burn the list.

What are some of the "cheap thrills" people commonly seek after? What are the cheap thrills that you find appealing?

What do you do when you find no pleasure in the material or spiritual world? (sleep, watch TV, etc.)

Is it easier for you to forgive others or to forgive yourself?

How do you use your guilt?

Prayer

God, I want to find all my happiness in you and your kingdom. Teach me to repent creatively instead of dragging my guilt with me everywhere. Amen.

40

The hope of God's promise

Revelation 21:1-4

Then I saw a new heaven and a new earth; for the first heaven and the first earth had passed away, and the sea was no more. And I saw the holy city, the new Jerusalem, coming down out of heaven from God, prepared as a bride adorned for her husband. And I heard a loud voice from the throne saying, "See, the home of God is among mortals. He will dwell with them as their God; they will be his peoples, and God himself will be with them; he will wipe every tear from their eyes. Death will be no more; mourning and crying and pain will be no more, for the first things have passed away."

When I first began assembling the biblical texts for this book, I debated whether to group them according to topic or in the order they appear in the Bible. I chose the biblical order and so this text from Revelation 21 came last. But even if it hadn't, I would have chosen to put it last, because I wanted to end on a note of hope. And I can think of no greater hope than that expressed in these four verses.

The Book of Revelation was written to support and encourage Christians suffering terrible persecution under a Roman emperor. We do not know with certainty which period of persecution it was written to address. Some hold that it was written just prior to 70 C.E. under the reign of Nero, who blamed the Christians for starting the great fire in Rome in order to deflect suspicion from himself. Consider the following account written by Tacitus, a historian unsympathetic to Christians:

> Nero inflicted the most exquisite tortures on a class hated for their abominations, called Christians by the populace. Christus from whom the name had its origin suffered the extreme penalty during the reign of Tiberius at the hands of one of our procurators, Pontius Pilatus, and a most mischievous superstition–again broke out not only in Judea, the first source of the evil, but even in Rome, where all things hideous and shameful from every part of the world find their centre and become popular. Accordingly, an immense multitude was convicted, not so much of the crime of firing the city, as of hatred against mankind. Mockery of every sort was added to their deaths. Covered with the skins of beasts, they were torn by dogs and perished, or were nailed to crosses, or were doomed to the flames and burnt, to serve as nightly illuminations when daylight had expired. Hence, even for criminals who deserve extreme and exemplary punishment, there arose a feeling of compassion; for it was not, as it seemed, for the public good, but to glut one man's extreme cruelty, that they were being destroyed (The New Testament Background: Selected Documents, edited by C. K. Barrett, Harper & Row, 1961, pp. 15-16).

Some place the date of Revelation toward the end of the first century C.E. under the reign of

Domitian, who instigated the first empire-wide persecution of Christians. Whatever the exact circumstances, the Christian readers for whom Revelation was intended were experiencing desperate times. Many had evidently become martyrs for their faith, and no doubt many were asking why God, whom they loved and served, did not intervene and save them.

The author of Revelation urged Christians to put their sufferings into the framework of history. The end times were near, he told them; their very sufferings showed that it was near. Christ was going to come soon and deal with the bullies who slandered, tortured, and killed them.

The text ends the section begun at 19:11, in which the author has seven visions concerning the end of Satan's age and the beginning of a new age under God's righteous rule. The words in 21:1-4 need little explanation. They echo somewhat another account of martyrs appearing before God's throne:

> Then one of the elders addressed me, saying, "Who are these, robed in white, and where have they come from?" I said to him, "Sir, you are the one that knows." Then he said to me, "These are they who have come out of the great ordeal; they have washed their robes and made them white in the blood of the Lamb. For this reason they are before the throne of God, and worship him day and night within his temple, and the one who is seated on the throne will shelter them. They will hunger no more, and thirst no more; the sun will not strike them, nor any scorching heat; for the Lamb at the center of the throne will be their

shepherd, and he will guide them to springs of the water of life, and God will wipe away every tear from their eyes" (Revelation 7:13-17).

Application

We may hesitate to compare ourselves to Christian martyrs. In fact, to compare our sufferings at all with the cruelty that the early Christians faced would seem conspicuously self-pitying. "These people were getting burned alive," we might tell ourselves, "and here I am whining about my marriage."

As a matter of fact, our situations and those of the early Christians do not compare. Some day, if we face persecution for our faith, if we find ourselves confronted with facing death for choosing to follow God, then we may turn to Revelation and read how our spiritual ancestors found themselves in similar straits.

What we can do with Revelation, however, is focus on the hope of God's promise. One day, this world will pass away, taking with it the great tragedies–the genocides and the holocausts, the famines and the wars–along with the petty evils that grind every person down.

Imagine. A world without unrequited love, without dysfunctional families, without office politics, without guilt, without anxieties, without loneliness. A world without depression.

Perhaps we will not even remember that depression once existed. How can shadowy memories of pain compete with the presence of God who will live among us? How can sadness find room within us when every nerve we possess hums with electric joy? When God wipes away our tears, will we forget that once upon a time and long ago, we wept?

You will be happy again. You won't have to wait until you die, either. Depression, like a broken bone, can be healed when treated properly. However, when fear and pain loom as an imminent reality instead of a dim memory, it is easy to forget that God is with us and God is for us and God loves us. Even when we doubt that we will ever feel whole again in this life, the thought of God's promise of a new age can sustain us, until it once again becomes easy to find hope.

Things to Think About

Do you expect Christ to return in your lifetime? How does this belief affect your spiritual life?

Do you find comfort in the thought of a new age when God will dwell among us? Or do you find the waiting for a new age intolerable?

Make a list of things you find most intolerable about your life. What would your life be like if they disappeared? What would your life be like if you did not remember they had ever existed?

Who are the people who experience the greatest suffering in this world? Is there anything you can do to alleviate that suffering, even on a smaller, more personal level?

Prayer

God, I believe in you and in your promise. Guide me on my journey until I return home to you. Amen.

Current research on depression and anxiety disorders

What follows is a brief overview of current medical research on depression. I have taken the information from an article entitled "Mood and Anxiety Disorders" in *Scientific American: Medicine*, eds. Edward Rubenstein and Daniel Federman (New York: Scientific American, Inc., 1991).

New medications and therapies are constantly being developed for mood disorders. The reader should not take the following information as the last word. Please also keep in mind that as Christians we have spiritual resources such as prayer, retreats, and pastoral counseling that can be used alone or in conjunction with other therapies.

Depression and mood disorders

The three most common mood disorders are major depression, dysthymic disorder (chronic milder depression), and bipolar disorder (sometimes called manic depression). At some point in their lives, about 10 percent of adults will experience one of these conditions.

We do not completely understand all the causes for depression. All types appear to run in families, with the genetic basis most clearly seen in bipolar disorders. Depression frequently appears as a complication of serious physical illnesses, such as heart disease and cancer. Drug and alcohol addictions can precipitate depression, and it can also be a side effect of many prescription drugs. Neurologic disorders, such as strokes and brain tumors, often result in depression, as well as certain metabolic disorders such as hyperthyroidism and diabetes mellitus.

The *DSM-III-R*, the standard diagnostic book for psychiatrists, gives the following criteria for diagnosing major depression. At least five of the following symptoms must occur nearly every day for a two-week period. Interestingly, if these criteria are the normal reaction to the death of a loved one, the *DSM-III-R* does not count it as major depression.

1. Depressed mood most of the day.

2. Diminished interest and pleasure in almost all activities.

3. Significant changes in weight or appetite.

4. Significant changes in sleep patterns.

5. An observation by others that one's movements and speech either seem to have slowed down or become more agitated.

6. Fatigue or loss of energy.

7. Feelings of worthlessness or excessive or inappropriate guilt.

8. Diminished ability to think, concentrate, or make decisions.

9. Recurrent thoughts of death (not just fear of death) and suicide.

People with dysthymia have many of the same symptoms listed above, but they tend to be less severe and last longer. They can be people who have never completely recovered from major depression or, more rarely, have some sort of personality disorder. True chronically depressed people often are regarded as pessimists and have low self-esteem. They go through life feeling generally unhappy or unwell.

Bipolar disorder is the rarest of the three basic types of depression. The key factor in diagnosing it lies in whether the person has manic symptoms (for example, inflated self-esteem, decreased need for sleep, increased talkativeness and distractibility, little regard for consequences of actions).

Treatments

Studies suggest that 70 to 80 percent of people with major depression (and without some other form of delusional mental illness) will respond to medication. Treatment normally continues for six months or more. Psychotherapy, either by itself or in conjunction with medication, is also helpful. Studies have shown that people with the most severe forms of depression respond better to medication than to psychotherapy.

Severely depressed people who cannot or will not take medication can be treated effectively with electroconvulsive therapy.

People with bipolar disorder are normally treated with medication and often require some in-patient hospital care.

Anxiety and panic disorders

Anxiety often occurs along with depression. It can be treated with antidepressants or sedatives, but often responds to cognitive behavioral therapy. This therapy helps people to think through why they feel frightened or anxious and see the situation for how it really is, instead of for how they fear it will be.

One of the most extreme manifestations of anxiety is the panic attack. According to the *DSM-III-R*, panic attacks are separate periods of intense fear and discomfort not triggered by a situation that would normally make any one fearful (for example, nearly getting involved in a car accident). A true panic attack has at least four of the following symptoms. When a person has one or two of the following conditions, it is called a "limited symptom attack":

1. Shortness of breath or a sensation of being smothered.
2. Dizziness, unsteadiness, or faintness.
3. Heart palpitations or rapid heartbeat.
4. Trembling or shaking.
5. Sweating.
6. Choking.
7. Nausea or abdominal discomfort.
8. Having an altered sense of self or reality.
9. Numbness or feeling a pricking, tingling, or creeping sensation on the skin.
10. Flushes or chills.
11. Chest pain or discomfort.
12. Fear of dying.
13. Fear of going crazy or losing control.

The anxiety of anticipating their next panic attack can paralyze people with a panic disorder (a repeated pattern of panic attacks). This anxiety is often more disabling than the actual panic attacks. Depression often results as a secondary diagnosis of a panic disorder. Panic disorders are highly responsive to treatment. A combination of cognitive therapy to treat the anxiety resulting from the panic attacks and antidepressant medications can be helpful.

Topical index

Numbers indicate which devotion deals with the topic.